laptop #7

# choke hold

### They Must Not Surrender to Fear's Grip

## by Christopher P.N. Maselli

Zonder**kidz**

*To Tina Davis for her creative support,
and whom, I think, isn't afraid of anything.*

# Zonder**kidz**®

*The children's group of Zondervan*

www.zonderkidz.com

*Choke Hold*
Copyright © 2004 by Christopher P. N. Maselli

Requests for information should be addressed to:
Zondervan, *Grand Rapids, Michigan 49530*

**Library of Congress Cataloging-in-Publication Data**

Maselli, Christopher P. N., 1971-
    Choke hold: they must not surrender to fear's grip / by Christopher P.N.
Maselli–1st ed.
      p. cm. –(The laptop series ; #7)
    Summary: Thirteen-year-old Matt is not supposed to use his laptop computer for two more weeks, but he is sure that using the computer's amazing power is the only way he will be able to keep Hulk Hooligan from maiming him on the wrestling mat.
    ISBN 0-310-70666-1 (pbk. : alk. paper)
    1. Computers—Fiction. 2. Wrestling—Fiction.
3. Christian life—Fiction. 4. Science fiction. I. Title.
PZ7.M3734Ch 2004
[Fic]–dc22
2003016980

*Editor: Gwen Ellis*
*Interior design: Beth Shagene and Todd Sprague*
*Art direction: Jody Langley*

*Printed in United States of America*

04 05 06 07 08 /❖DC/ 10 9 8 7 6 5 4 3 2 1

# Contents

# Spinning Around

*Discovering truth puts fear to rest. One inventor had discovered the truth long ago about those who stole her invention. Now it was time to share that truth with the only person who could stop the evil from happening again...a teenage boy who was wrestling with challenges of his own.*

Flashes of blue, red, white, yellow, and black. Flashes of light and concrete. Flashes of his life up until now.

As thirteen-year-old Matt Calahan spun through the air, his arms and feet flailing like a puppet's, flashes were all his mind could process. Well, flashes and three words: "I hate wrestliiiiiing!!!"

*Ker-thump!* Hulk Hooligan stopped spinning Matt around as if he was a set of helicopter blades ... and let him drop to the ground. Matt's body hit the canvas like rubber, bouncing up slightly before coming to rest.

"Tails!" someone shouted. "I told you he'd land face down!"

Matt rolled over slightly, his head still spinning. He tugged at a few strands of wet, black hair which were plastered to his forehead.

"No one messes wit' da *Hooligan!*" Hulk gloated to his classmates.

Matt's eyes nearly crossed as the two-hundred-and-something-pound-bully-with-bleached-hair hooted and hollered and growled like a rabid dog.

 Matt grimaced, pushed his torso up, and pulled his knees to his chest. Then he lifted his head.

Hulk Hooligan frowned. "Ah, ya want summore, Calhan?"

"Cal-*a*-han," Matt growled back, pushing himself into a kneeling position.

"Arrraugh!" Hulk shouted, coming at Matt with his meaty hands leading.

Matt dodged to the side, half rolling, half sliding. Still crouched, he popped his chest up, his arms out, ready for Hulk's next move.

"How much more o' this can ya take?" Hulk taunted.

*Not much more*, Matt thought.

From the crowd, Matt's best friend Alfonzo shouted, "How much more can you give, Hulk?"

Matt's other two best friends, Lamar and Gill, laughed at Alfonzo's challenge to the big guy. Matt groaned. He'd have to talk to Alfonzo.

Hulk shot forward. Matt shot to the left. Hulk shot to the left. Matt shot to the right.

"Go, Matt!" Lamar shouted.

"Just don't let him land on you!" Gill warned.

Hulk ran to the side of the mat and picked up Coach Plymouth's chair, which was empty because the coach had gone to the bathroom. Which was fine, except he had left just as Matt and Hulk met on the mat. Which wasn't so great. Hulk lifted the chair in the air.

"How many times do I have to tell you?" Matt pleaded. "This is junior high wrestling—*not* the WWE!"

"What's da difference?" Hulk aimed the rungs of the chair toward Matt, then froze when the high-pitched scream of a whistle echoed off the gymnasium walls.

Coach Plymouth ran up to the boys, waving his arms. The whistle dropped from his mouth when he stepped onto the mat. "The difference," he said gruffly to Hulk, "is that in junior high wrestling, we don't use *chairs*."

Hulk put the chair down, nodding, as if the coach had spoken a revelation.

Matt let out a slow breath. He pinched himself to see if he was really still alive, then stumbled over and crashed to the floor beside Lamar, Gill, and Alfonzo. He crossed his legs underneath him, while pulling a towel out of his gym bag and wiping off his face.

Gill wrinkled his nose. "You stink," he whispered.

"I've been wrestling." Matt wiped under his arms with his towel. "What are you doing here anyway? You're not in our gym class."

"I'm scouting," Gill said.

"In other words," Lamar leaned in, "no one needs any A/V services today."

Gill smiled. He *always* had the run of the school during the hour he was supposed to be helping deliver TVs and VCRs from one classroom to another. He finished his job in about five minutes and used the rest of the time to pal around.

 "No, I'm serious." Gill bobbed his head left to right. "I've decided to get out of show business and get into management. That's where the real chunk-o-change is. C'mon, let me be your manager."

"Oh brother." Matt stuffed his towel in his bag.

"Now, c'mon, you don't really hate wrestling, do you?"

"No. What I hate is getting beat up."

Gill nodded. "A manager could help you work on that." He pointed to Matt's neck. "You missed a spot."

"Well, boys, I've got a surprise for you," Coach Plymouth announced, standing in the middle of the wrestling mat. His jumpsuit was tightly stretched across his belly. He waited, but no one responded, and so he continued. "There's a reason we've been studying wrestling in gym class. And there's a reason we're going to continue studying it for the next couple weeks."

The class of boys just stared at the coach. Matt's eyes drifted over to the girls on the other side of the gym. They were bouncing a multicolored beach ball on a gigantic parachute. *How is it that they get to play the safe games?* he wondered.

"The reason we're studying wrestling," Coach said, "is because I want to start a team!"

"Shweet!" Hulk punched his fist into his palm.

Some of the guys chuckled.

"Er . . . yeah, it is pretty, uh, *shweet*. Anyway, I want to see potential here," Coach said, emphasizing the word "potential." "That's the key. *Potential*. I can train you later. Just show me you've got what it takes to be a wrestler."

The boys looked at each other.

"Now in an actual meet, you would wrestle for three periods, one to two minutes each. But this is gym class, and I want to see you guys wrestle. So we'll just wrestle for three minutes each time, got it?"

Several heads nodded.

"Finally, in a couple weeks, I'm going to pit you against one another and keep track of the scores. I'm making up the chart now. Don't worry—we're not going to weigh in or anything. Not yet. I just want you guys to wrestle each other. That means, at times, big guys and little guys could be in a match together. That's the breaks. But like I said, I'm not looking for winners. I'm looking for potential. I'll try to keep it as fair as possible."

Matt's eyes darted to Hulk. *Interesting choice of words,* he thought, massaging his sore arm. *"That's the breaks." If I have another bout with "da Hooligan," and he's not fooling around, breaks are sure to happen.*

"Look at this bruise on my arm," Matt pointed out to his friends. Just below his shoulder, his arm was tinted black and blue.

In the Enisburg Junior High School locker room, Matt, Lamar, and Alfonzo had showered and were now getting dressed again for the remainder of the school day. Gill leaned against the lockers, punching numbers into a calculator.

Lamar surveyed Matt's bruise and shook his head. "Man, that's gonna get dark."

"At least Hulk didn't snap it," Alfonzo said.

Matt gulped. "Snap it?"

"I'm just kidding," Alfonzo said, rolling on his deodorant.

"I think I'm lucky to be alive."

"It wasn't that bad," Lamar chided.

"Actually," Gill said, looking up, "from where I was sitting, it *was* pretty bad."

Matt looked at Gill, the red-haired comedian. "Thanks for the support."

"Anytime, my friend. A manager is always honest with the little people under him."

"Little people?! Hey, at least *I* didn't throw up on him."

"Hey, ya gotta do what works for you."

Suddenly the bench shook.

"Speaking of . . ."

Hulk rounded the corner. He looked at Matt's bruised arm and chuckled. "Nice battle wound, Calhan."

"What's your problem?" Matt challenged the big guy. "Did you have to be so dramatic out there?"

"If I member right, ya didn't keep yer promise to me. Ya promised to help me become fit."

"It's impossible."

"Shuddup."

"Look, I've tried. I've told you that you have to exercise every day. And diet."

"Forget all dat. I just wanna be in shape for da tournament."

"Exercise. Diet."

Hulk huffed. His eyes cut to Alfonzo, then back to Matt. "Okay, gimme a list or somethin' of what I gotta eat."

Gill piped up, "Hey, Hulk, you looking for a manager?"

"Gill!" Matt shouted.

"What? Did you see him out there? He clobbered you."

"So now you're not going to be *my* manager?"

"You want me to be your manager?" Gill asked, looking hopeful.

"Well, ya ain't gonna be *my* manager," Hulk said to Gill. "I need someone with brains."

"Oh sure," Gill countered. "You think Matt has brains just because he wears glasses."

Matt blinked. "I don't wear glasses."

Gill looked at Matt for a long moment, then turned back to Hulk. "What do you say?"

Hulk shook his head. "I say," he leaned into Matt's face, "if Matt don't help me get fit, next time we're in da ring together, I'm gonna beat da snot outta him." On that note, he stepped back and went to pick on someone else smaller than him.

Matt gulped and pushed Gill. "You'll be his manager?"

"What?"

"I'm gonna get the snot beat outta me, that's what."

"That's really a gross visual," Gill said. "But how is this any different than the other hundred times?"

"Because," Matt said, looking around. "You know."

"Oh!" Gill's eyes grew big. "Because you don't have the laptop this time!"

"Shhh!" Matt, Lamar, and Alfonzo all shushed him.

"Yes, that's right," Matt admitted. "I'm still grounded from it."

"Well, do you know where it is?" Alfonzo asked in his only-slightly-Spanish accent.

Matt looked at Lamar, who just raised his dark eyebrows.

"Yeah, I know where it is," Matt told them.

It was shoved under a shoebox on the top shelf of his dad's closet. It had been nearly two weeks now since his dad took it away. His reasons were understandable—because they were true. He thought Matt was spending *way* too much time on his laptop and not enough time doing anything else . . . like sports . . . like wrestling. But his dad didn't understand. He didn't know when be bought it for Matt's thirteenth birthday that this laptop was special. Matt had quickly discovered this was no ordinary computer. This laptop—somehow, someway—could make whatever Matt typed into it actually *happen*. Of course, this made the laptop not only very powerful, but also very dangerous. In a way, Matt was relieved to be away from it for a short while. Still . . . it would be awfully nice to have it so that he could avoid any trouble with Hulk—and *certainly* to keep him off the same wrestling mat.

There was also the matter of Sam—the laptop's previous owner who had recently told Matt she needed his help. She still freaked him out sometimes. But with the laptop stored away, for the last couple weeks she was nowhere to be seen.

"So . . ." Alfonzo pressed.

"So . . ." Matt repeated.

"So why don't you just sneak in and use it?"

Matt, Lamar, and Gill looked at each other.

"Hey, man," Lamar spoke up, "that's not cool. Matt's grounded from it. As a Christian, he can't do that. It's not right."

"Not to mention that I'd get in *huge* trouble," Matt added.

Alfonzo shrugged. "Hey, this Christian stuff is all new to me. Sorry. Seems like life would be easier without all these rules, though."

"No one said being a Christian was easy," Lamar said, always the one to make a spiritual point. "If anything, it's hard to be a Christian. It's much easier to live without any standards."

"Yeah," Matt agreed, tying his tennis shoe. "We live by a higher standard."

Alfonzo shrugged again.

"Besides," Matt added, "I would get in *huge* trouble."

"So I've heard."

"Hey Matt!" Coach Plymouth blurted out as he rounded the corner.

The four boys jumped and Matt nearly fell over. "Yes, Coach?"

"I need to see you in my office."

"In trouble again, Matt?" Gill whispered as the coach walked away. "See, if you had a manager, you could avoid snags like this."

Matt entered Coach Plymouth's office, softly closing the door behind him. He wanted to beat the coach to the punch, asking, "What'd *I* do?" but he kept his mouth shut. Gill had gone off to deliver another TV to a class and Alfonzo had headed for his math class. Lamar, with just a study hall ahead, had promised to stick around outside for support. Matt hoped he was out there praying.

Coach Plymouth was perched on the edge of his desk, leaning up against the pile of paperwork in his inbox. His office seemed rather dark with the blinds drawn. Coach's computer displayed an Arizona Cardinals screensaver. A gold trophy shaped like a football sat at one corner of his desk, next to a glass of water that had to be at least 44 ounces. He took a chug of the water and then set the glass back down.

"So I guess you're wondering why I called you in here," the coach barked.

"I didn't do it," Matt said, only half-kidding.

The coach laughed. "You're not in trouble."

Matt felt the tension release.

"No, in fact, just the opposite."

Matt felt the tension return.

 "I've been watching you, Matt, and I really want you to try your hardest for our wrestling team. When I was talking about potential out there, I was talking about *you.*"

Matt looked behind him. Nope, he was the only one in the room. "Me?"

Coach Plymouth nodded. "You're fast and you're smart. That's the kind of wrestler I need."

"But . . . I'm not . . . big."

"Bulk is only one piece of the puzzle," Coach said like a teacher.

Matt felt his mouth dry up as he considered this. Then he took a shot in the dark. "Did my dad call you?"

Coach Plymouth smiled. "No, this is all me. Though I've talked to your dad before and I know he'd love for you to find a sport you liked."

"He said that?"

"All dads say that."

Matt's mind rushed as he contemplated being thrown onto the wrestling mat again and again, against bigger, stronger guys than himself. He saw blue and black becoming his best colors. But then again, if *Coach* thought Matt could do it, maybe he could. He did *enjoy* wrestling—except for when he had wrestled Hulk—but he never thought he'd be on a team. He wasn't too good at too many sports, but maybe this time he could be. That would really be *something*.

"Me?" Matt said again.

"Think about it, Matt." Coach Plymouth walked back around his desk and sat down in his high-back chair. "I think you've got what it takes. Will you give it your best shot?"

Matt envisioned himself slamming his opponent down on the mat for the count. He saw his teammates carrying him on their shoulders, fireworks in the distance, confetti littering his hair. He saw the other team crying like babies because they got crushed on the mat *by* the Matt. He saw his friends cheering. He saw Alfonzo's sister, Isabel, clapping joyfully at his triumph. Then he saw his parents smiling, his dad giving him a thumbs up.

Matt smiled and suddenly found himself saying, "Yeah, sure. It would be cool to be on the team."

Coach Plymouth nodded happily, swiveled in his chair, and started typing. Matt waited for him to dismiss him, but after a minute, realized he must have already done so. Matt slowly turned around and exited as quietly as he had entered.

On the other side of the door, Lamar stopped pacing. His brown eyes were as big as Frisbees. "What happened?"

Still dumbfounded, Matt pulled the door shut and gulped. "Let's just say, now I *really* need the laptop."

"But your parents grounded you."

Matt twisted his lip and looked straight at Lamar. "I know. . .but maybe I can talk them out of it."

# The Con Game

## 2

"That's great, Ace!" Stan Calahan, Matt's father snapped his gum and slapped Matt on the back. A broad-shouldered man with a square jaw, he was always chewing gum like it was going out of style. Today he wore his signature plaid shirt and blue jeans.

Matt grimaced. "Yeah, it'd be cool, though I don't know—"

"We're really proud of you," Matt's mother, Penny Calahan, agreed. She wore jeans also, with a pink blouse that brought out her soft facial features and contrasted with her short, straight black hair.

Matt's parents were suddenly into spring cleaning, shifting boxes and gadgets around inside the garage. Matt's dad popped open a box and shuffled through it.

"Well," Matt continued, "Coach says he wants me on the team, but I don't know if I'll actually make—"

"Oh, don't worry about it," Mr. Calahan said, looking up with a wink. "You'll do great. This could be right up your alley."

"But I'm not really stro—"

"Oh!" Mrs. Calahan interjected. "And girls like boys with vision. Boys who are able to take on a challenge with gusto!"

"Mom! Believe me. I'm not trying to impress girls."

Penny Calahan's dark eyebrows popped up. "None?"

Matt sat down on a nearby step and looked at the concrete floor. He thought of Alfonzo's sister, Isabel, living across the street, with the midnight black hair that cascaded down her back like a waterfall, and the voice that sounded like newly-spun honey. He swallowed. "Mom, I'm not—"

"Oh, she's just a hopeless romantic." Matt's dad leaned over and pecked his wife on the cheek.

Her right hand flew up. "Guilty!" she sang.

"But seriously," Mr. Calahan said, his attention back in his box. "Wrestling will be good for you. Might distract you from that laptop."

Matt looked up from the step he was sitting on and brushed a strand of hair out of his eyes. "Heh. Uh . . . yeah." He sat still for a few moments, mustering his courage. Finally, he blurted out, "So can I have it back? I've been grounded for nearly two weeks and been *really* good."

Mr. Calahan set down his box. He looked at Matt and pointedly said, "No."

"But—"

"No, Matt. Our agreement was four weeks away from the laptop. It was consuming you—like you couldn't live without it. That's not healthy."

"Pleeeeeeeeeeease?"

Matt's mom laughed. "Like that's gonna work."

"It works."

"When you were *two* it worked. Matt, you're a teenager now. We expect you to be responsible."

Matt rolled his eyes. Yes, he was a teenager now. That's what had started all this trouble—turning thirteen and receiving an amazing laptop for his birthday. "I *am* responsible!" he cried.

"And you're going to be responsible for two more weeks," Matt's dad added.

"But—"

"Look, you've got nothing to fear as long as you keep up a good attitude about it. You'll have your laptop back in two weeks."

"But what if I need it before then?"

"Use a pad and paper," Penny Calahan suggested.

"It's not the same, believe me," Matt said dryly. His knee started moving up and down. *Nothing to fear.* That's what his dad had said. He had nothing to fear. But his dad didn't know that there was *no way* to ensure his safety—or even his place on the wrestling team—without a little nudge from the laptop. He needed an edge. He needed to be *sure* Hulk couldn't pound him to a pulp.

"Are you absolutely, positively sure?" Matt tried again.

"Matt," Stan Calahan said, his tone of voice becoming a warning.

"No way I can convince you?"

"It would take some pretty hard convincing, Ace."

## Con #1

In his bedroom, Matt reclined on his bed, cordless phone in hand. He stared up at his ceiling light, opening and closing his eyes, watching red spots appear out of nowhere. Gill was on the other end of the line, trying his best to help.

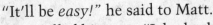

"It'll be *easy!*" he said to Matt.

Matt rolled his eyes. "I doubt that. I practically begged my dad to give me my laptop back and he said it's not gonna happen."

"Well, that's because you're trying to do this without your manager."

"Oh, you want to try?"

"Can I be your manager?"

"I'm not paying you anything, Gill."

"I'll do this pro bono."

"So now you're my lawyer, too?"

"What's the difference? Look, all you have to do is be a salesman."

Matt lifted the phone away from his ear and looked at it. He pulled it back. "How's that?"

"Well," Gill said, "the first thing you learn in sales is that you have to get the customer saying 'yes.' You get them saying 'yes, yes, yes' and you can get them to do anything you want."

"Are you sure about that?"

"I have an uncle in sales. He's a telemarketer. You know, sales by phone."

"You're gonna have him call my dad during dinner?"

"*No,*" Gill corrected, as if the notion was ridiculous. "I'll do it. You have three-way calling, right?"

"Yeah."

"So put me on with your dad's cell phone."

"Now?"

"Yeah."

Matt shrugged. *It can't hurt.*

"Hold on." Matt sat up and dialed his dad's cellular phone number from memory. Two rings later, his dad—just downstairs—answered his cell phone.

"Stan Calahan," he said boldly.

Matt quickly clicked Gill on the line.

"Stan Calahan," Matt's dad said again. "Hello?"

"Mr. Calahan!" Gill shouted, his voice deep and robust, sounding quite a bit like Mr. Moviefone. "May I have a moment of your time?"

"No, I—"

"Good!"

*Way to go*, Matt thought. *Get him saying 'no' right away.*

Gill continued, "You've been selected as a winner here at K-L-M-N-O-P Radio!"

"I ... I have?"

"Yes! Yes! Yes! Er ... could you please turn your radio down? We're getting feedback."

After a short pause, Matt's dad said, "I don't have a radio on."

Matt winced.

"Right!" Gill said quickly. "Must be short waves from the Aurora Bor ... er ... Northern Lights!"

"Aren't they ... up North?"

"So all you have to do," Gill pressed Matt's dad, "is answer three simple questions and you could win your choice of a thousand dollars or an off-season trip to Cancun. Sound good?"

"Er ... yes?"

"Yes!"

Matt closed his eyes and crashed back onto his pillow.

"Question one," Gill started. "Does the earth revolve around the sun?"

"Yes."

"Yes! Two: Do yellow and blue make green?"

"Yes."

"Yes! Is *Attack of the Clones* better than *The Phantom Menace*?"

"Yes."

"Yes! And now for our final question: Can Matt have his laptop back?"

Matt sat up in bed, the phone pressed to his ear.

"That's *four* questions, Gill," Matt's dad said, "and the answer's no."

*Click!*

## Con #2

"What . . . what's *this*?" Matt's mother asked, entering the kitchen after a long day at work.

"Dinner for you and dad," Matt said warmly.

The table was set with clean plates, polished silverware, long-stem glasses and a bouquet of paper flowers Matt created out of old Nickelodeon magazine pages. He didn't dare pick any of his mom's flowers out back.

A peppery, saucy smell lingered in the air; two Salisbury steaks were baking in the oven, along with peas, candied apples, and whatever else was in the Swanson dinner trays.

"This is so sweet, honey!" Penny Calahan cheered, hugging Matt. "Does your dad know?"

"I called him and told him to come home early for a special dinner."

"How about that."

Matt smiled. He took his mother's coat and brief-case and told her to have a seat at the table. A moment later, Matt returned to the kitchen with a boom box. He plugged it in and spun up a classical music CD. Beethoven was about halfway through his "Moonlight Sonata" when Matt's dad popped open the door from the garage and entered the kitchen.

"Look what Matt prepared us!" Mrs. Calahan exclaimed.

Stan Calahan smiled and nodded and handed his coat to Matt, who promptly left to hang it in the hall closet. He returned, lit two candles, and placed them in the center of the table.

"Very romantic," Matt's mother said.

"Very," his dad replied, smiling at her, a twinkle in his eye.

With flower-print oven mitts, Matt pulled out the dinners, arranged them on plates, and set them in front of his parents.

"Aren't you going to eat?" Matt's mother asked.

"Naw," Matt declined. "I'll grab something later when I clean up."

"You're going to clean up, too? This is so sweet, honey. Isn't this sweet, Stan?"

"It is." His dad looked at him closely. Then he ruffed up Matt's hair. "And you know what? You're still not getting the laptop."

## Con #3

After dinner, as Matt predicted to himself, his father retired to the living room and sat back in his La-Z-Boy. Matt watched him search for the remote and finally turn on the TV by hand. Matt stood around the corner with the remote in hand. On the Enisburg news station, the weatherman finished up the forecast. Two commercials followed. Then, right after sta- 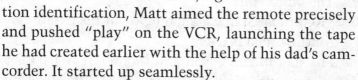 tion identification, Matt aimed the remote precisely and pushed "play" on the VCR, launching the tape he had created earlier with the help of his dad's camcorder. It started up seamlessly.

On the television screen, Matt popped up behind a makeshift desk, brow furled, in a blue suit with a red tie. Gill had promised it was the best combination for TV.

"Today's story," said Matt's on-screen persona, "is about a young man who was denied an outlet for his creativity. This is the story of Matt Calahan." Matt-at-the-news-desk held up a family photo of himself. Matt-in-the-hallway smiled. "Yes, this is the young man who had a bright future as the greatest writer of all time. He was so great, he didn't even need an editor."

The screen flashed to Matt standing in a trench coat with a mustache stuck on his upper lip. "I'm an editor," Matt-the-trenchcoat-wearing-editor said. "I'm outta work."

The screen flashed back to Matt-at-the-news-desk. "But that bright future has changed . . . because his laptop was taken away."

"Matt!!" Matt's dad shouted.

The real Matt put on a wide, cheesy smile and rounded the corner. *Please,* he thought, *please give me the laptop back!*

"Remote." Stan Calahan held out his hand.

Matt handed it over.

His dad pushed stop and looked at Matt for a long moment. "I thought you once told me that *everyone* needs an editor—no matter how good they write."

"Oh sure," Matt admitted, "*now*. But I was planning to change all that."

Mr. Calahan kept a straight face. "This," he said, "is why you're grounded from your laptop. You seem to think that without it, your life won't be the same. It's just a laptop."

"It's not . . . well . . . it's just really important. My future, Dad."

"Hogwash, Matt," his dad said, pointedly. "You can wait. Just two more weeks."

"But . . . what if it's really important?"

"It won't be."

"But what if it is . . . a matter of life and death?"

Matt's dad looked at Matt for a long time, as if trying to read his thoughts. Then, "Right, sure," he said flatly, "if it's a matter of life and death. But, Matt—"

Matt raised his eyebrows.

"I can't imagine one instance where typing a story means the difference between life or death. So no more begging or it'll be longer."

Matt kept his mouth shut and exited the room. It was times like this he wished he could just tell his dad all about the laptop's special power to literally change the future. But he knew he couldn't. It was too dangerous. Matt and his friends had decided to keep it a secret to protect the ones they loved. And now that secret meant Matt was about to "have the snot beat out of him." Gill was right. It was a less than pleasant visual.

Matt sighed. It *was* a matter of life and death and his dad just didn't realize the laptop could make all the difference. He just didn't understand.

"My dad just doesn't understand," Matt told Lamar, Gill, and Alfonzo at school the next day.

"I can't believe you actually thought you could talk him out of it," Lamar said.

"I didn't have much of a choice." Matt held a small stack of notebook paper out. "Look at all this stuff I've had to research for Hulk. It's my only hope now for saving my life." He stuffed the wad of papers into his backpack.

"Well, you shouldn't have agreed to help Hulk then," Alfonzo said.

"Believe me, I didn't have a choice about that either."

The friends had made their way from the school-yard into the school foyer when Matt heard a faint whisper that made him freeze in place.

Noticing Matt stop, Lamar stopped too, and turned around. "What?"

"You didn't hear that?"

"Hear what?" Lamar said.

"I don't . . ."

There! Matt heard it again. A faint whisper . . . like a child straining to say . . .

*"Wordtronix!"*

Matt turned around. The whisper was coming from out in the schoolyard. But who would know the name "Wordtronix"—the unique, untraceable brand of his laptop?

"I'm . . . I'll be right in," Matt told his friends.

Lamar looked at Matt quizzically, then shrugged and said he'd see him in class. Matt stepped out of the foyer and back into the schoolyard. He cut down the side of the brick school building and made his way past a few long windows. He stopped and listened.

Nothing.

He moved farther.

Still nothing.

At the corner of the building, he stopped one more time to listen. But with all Matt's schoolmates now inside the schoolyard had grown quiet.

Matt scratched his head. There was no one in sight. *Must be imagining things.*

Matt swiveled to return to the foyer when a gloved hand grabbed the back of his coat and yanked him around the side of the building.

# Bein' Sneaky

## 3

Stupid, stupid, stupid!" Matt said to himself as he waited behind the Happy Gas gas station, a few blocks from his house. He shifted his backpack on his shoulder and felt the weight of the laptop inside shift. He shook his head. He would be in *so much* trouble if his parents found out he had taken the laptop out of their closet.

He didn't want to do it.

He almost didn't do it.

But he did it.

Because Sam insisted.

Sam, the previous owner of the laptop, knew *everything* about it—much more than she had ever shared with Matt. She was mysterious in every way. To this day, Matt hadn't even seen her face or heard her true voice. She was always strategically cloaked in the dark or concealed in the shadows, so Matt and his friends couldn't get a glimpse of her.

Even earlier that day at school, when she had pulled him around the side of the building and told him to meet her here, she had kept her face hidden beneath a dark 40s-style hat ... and she still spoke using some kind of electronic device that distorted her voice. Gill always said her voice sounded like Darth Vader's, except higher pitched. Matt agreed.

It hurt his gut to disobey his parents and go through with sneaking the laptop out of the house. Normally, Matt wouldn't have even entertained such a request. He *knew* it was wrong. But Sam said it was urgent. She said lives could depend on it. So Matt felt he had no choice, because Sam had no reason to lie. Matt understood that the mystery of Sam and the laptop was greater  than he was ... greater than his world. Still, that didn't make it any easier. It *was* still wrong to do. But Matt didn't want anyone to suffer because of the laptop, and after months of secrets and danger, he was truthfully ready to discover some answers. So here he stood, at the back of Happy Gas, trying to ignore the fuel fumes that tickled his nose. His bike was propped up against the building, and he continued to wait, albeit against his better judgment.

"Hello, Matt," the raspy, female voice behind him spoke.

Matt jumped, then spun around, instinctively balling his fists.

There she stood: A tall, blonde-haired woman in a black trench coat and 40s-style hat.

Matt squinted. "Do I . . ."

"It's me, Matt. It's Sam."

Matt's jaw dropped. Sam . . . without the shadows, without the masks. It was the same trench coat. The same hat. Even the same thin black boots.

He could hear her voice now—for real—and see her face. Her eyes were hazel; her face long and free of makeup. Her hair was straight, dropping down just past her shoulders, where it rested in soft curls.

Matt gulped. "How . . . how do I know it's you?"

Sam smirked. "You were meeting someone else here?"

Matt looked around. "Well . . . no."

Matt's eyes darted to Sam's right cheek. From the cheekbone to the center of her neck, her skin was a lighter color—almost bleach-white—with light, scarring ripples as though it were the aftermath of an old burn.

Sam stepped back and placed her black-gloved hand on her cheek. "Ugliness," she said.

"Oh!" Matt's eyes grew wide, realizing she had caught his gaze. "No—"

"I mean it *came* from ugliness. From the past."

Matt blinked and looked at the pavement. He wasn't sure what to say.

"I'm sorry," Sam said. "I didn't mean to make you uncomfortable."

Matt dismissed the thought. "You have no idea," he said. "Ever since I got the laptop, 'uncomfortable' has been a way of life."

"I know. And I'm sorry, Matt."

There was a long, awkward pause, until Sam asked, "You brought the laptop?"

"Yeah. But I shouldn't even have it with me. I had to steal it out of my own house."

"What?"

"I'm grounded from it right now. This is wrong on *so many* levels."

Sam looked at Matt for a long moment, her hazel eyes sunken in worry. "It's for the greater good, Matt. If your parents knew, they'd understand. But you're doing the right thing, keeping it a secret."

"I know. I understand I had to. . .but I'm not doing the right thing, stealing it out of my own house."

Sam moved forward, to place a hand on Matt's shoulder, but Matt scooted back. Sam said, "It's okay, so long as no one gets hurt. That's what we're trying to prevent . . . anyone from getting hurt."

Matt walked a few steps away then turned to Sam. "*What* are we trying to prevent?" he demanded. "You keep coming to me in secret, telling me only bits of the story. I have no idea what's going on."

"You'll know soon enough, Matt, I promise. Really—I've been trying to protect you."

Seeing Sam for the first time here, Matt thought she looked weaker than he expected. Just a young woman who had been sentenced to creeping around in shadows.

"Thank you for getting rid of the disguise," Matt said.

"I want you to trust me," she said. "I'll do whatever it takes. We need each other."

After a pause, Matt pulled off his backpack. "It's in here."

"Let's boot it up."

Matt nodded. He unzipped his backpack and pulled out the laptop; its thin, black casing glimmered in the sun. Sam stepped back and gasped slightly. Matt realized this was the first time she had seen it in a very long time. Her eyes were fixed on it. Still standing, Matt pressed the power button with one hand as he balanced it atop the other. Together they waited.

"What do you mean, we need each other?" Matt asked as the Wordtronix logo spun on-screen.

"You need me—to make the danger go away," she told him. "And I need you . . . to do the same." Sam slowly reached forward, her fingers inching toward the plastic laptop casing. She nearly touched it, but then trembled and pulled away.

Matt smirked. "This isn't *Lord of the Rings*," he said.

Sam's eyebrows lifted.

With the laptop fully booted, Matt asked, "What now?"

"I need you to pull up the file on the CD."

Matt looked at Sam blank-faced.

"The CD," Sam repeated, "the one you said you found in my underground lab."

Matt closed the laptop's lid. "You didn't tell me to *bring* the CD."

"You didn't bring the CD?"

"Did you say, 'Bring the CD?' No, you said, 'Bring the *laptop*.'"

"Well, I just assumed . . ."

"I don't believe this."

"Can you go home and get it?"

Matt looked at his watch. "I can't get back in time. I have youth group tonight. I'm pushing it as it is."

Sam thought for a moment, then instructed, "Meet me back here in three days."

Matt slipped open the laptop's lid and powered the computer down. Unbelievable. All this drama—for nothing. And now he would have to steal the laptop from his parents' closet a *second* time.

He sighed. "Is this really necessary? Right now? Is this really a matter of life and death?"

"More than you know, Matt."

"I've seen the CD. The only thing on it is a picture of a gray blob." A *bunch* of gray blobs, to be exact.

"I know. I need to see it. Verify its contents. It's the first step . . . to the last."

Matt stared at Sam in disbelief. "I have no idea what you're talking about."

"You will. I promise."

"Fine. Three days. But this better be as important as you say it is."

Sam nodded, then turned, her trench coat whipping around like a cape.

"Sam!" Matt cried before she disappeared.

 The young woman with the sad hazel eyes peered back over her shoulder.

"You're not ugly, Sam," he said. "You're just scarred."

Before youth group started, Lamar scratched on a pad of paper with his pencil

Matt pursed his lips. Lamar had drawn a pencil-sketch from Matt's description of Sam. It looked pretty accurate, too. He knew Lamar was a good artist, but he hadn't seen him draw many real people. This sketch did look like a real person, all right.

"I don't see why you're so on edge," he said to Matt, pointing at his sketch. "She doesn't look that dangerous to me."

"Yeah," Gill said, "she looks normal enough to me. How old you think she is? We could fix her up with Alfonzo's dad."

"No, thanks," Alfonzo said flatly, from the other side of Gill.

"I guess she's probably like twenty-five or so. Maybe thirty-five, forty."

Lamar, Gill, and Alfonzo looked at Matt dubiously.

"Okay, so I'm not good at ages," Matt admitted.

"She looks about thirty-something to me," Lamar said, studying his drawing. "Man, that's sad. Thirty-something and she's stuck in hiding."

"I have a feeling we don't know the half of it," Matt said, looking over his shoulder.

Several guys occupied the back rows of the room. They were the ones who didn't really want to be there—guys like Hulk Hooligan—who always slouched in their chairs, made fun of Pastor Ruhlen, and talked about girls.

Matt's observations were interrupted when Pastor Ruhlen took the stage

"Dudes!" he shouted. This was always the way he said "hello." "Welcome to 2:52—where we learn to grow smarter, stronger, deeper, and cooler, like Jesus. In Luke 2:52, it says Jesus grew in wisdom and stature, and in favor with God and men. So let's do-to-do it!"

Lamar closed his sketchpad and shoved it under his chair. The boys stood up and sang a chorus with Pastor Ruhlen on guitar. Matt glanced over to the other side of the room, where most of the girls sat. The boys on the left, the girls on the right. It just sort of happened that way every week—Matt wasn't sure why. He could see Alfonzo's sister, Isabel, sitting about halfway back, singing along. He looked toward the back of the room again. Sure enough, the big, "too cool for this stuff" guys were slouched in their chairs, not participating. Matt looked at their arms. They were *huge.* They were the kind of guys Matt might have to wrestle. They were twice his strength and size and even had bits of facial hair. Matt shuddered. They probably used straight-edged, triple-blade razors.

After a few songs and announcements, Pastor Ruhlen began his message. "Tonight, I'm speaker-ino-ing on fear. Dudes! Do you know you don't have to live in fear?"

*Yeah*, Matt thought, *but then again*, you *don't have to wrestle the Incredible Hulks.*

"What is bothering you?" Lamar whispered to Matt. "You've seen Sam a bunch of times."

Gill leaned over and put the back of his hand on Lamar's chest. "As Matt's manager, I think I should be the one to handle this."

"Gill!" Lamar scolded.

"So Matt," Gill said, giving Lamar a disapproving glance. "What is bothering you? You've seen Sam a bunch of times."

Matt looked up at Pastor Ruhlen. He was preaching from the other side of the stage.

"Sam's not bothering me," Matt admitted. "What bothers me is that without the laptop's help, I'm sunk in wrestling."

"C'mon, Matt. That's not true. Remember—you made it through football without the laptop."

"I mean," Matt clarified, "I could end up with more bruises like these." He pointed to his shoulder, which still throbbed and was blacker-and-bluer than ever.

"Well, duh," Gill said.

Lamar pushed Gill away, saying, "It comes with the territory. You just need to decide if you want to be on the team or not."

Matt shrugged. "Well, yeah. Coach thinks I can do it. I thought it might be cool."

"It *is* cool."

Matt looked over his shoulder again. "But is it worth the risk?"

"What risk?" Lamar asked. "It's not a matter of life and death. You're talking bruises—*if* that. It's not nearly as rough as football was—and you did fine."

"He made touchdowns for the other team, remember," Gill interjected.

Matt huffed. "Look, in football, I just wanted to look like I knew what I was doing. In wrestling, yeah, I want to do *good*. But I also want to make it through with all my body parts in tact. I think wrestling is a *lot* more dangerous."

"More dangerous than football?"

"Yes—because I'm *against* guys like Hulk this time. At least in football, Hulk was on my team."

Lamar shook his head. "You're talking in circles."

"Oh, and did I tell you Sam had me bring the laptop to her?"

Lamar's mouth dropped open.

Gill leaned forward. "What!" he shouted.

Alfonzo turned. "Shhh!"

Pastor Ruhlen stopped speaking and cut his eyes to the boys. He was a lanky man with hair that resembled a Chia-pet. Today it was bright yellow. Tomorrow it would be a different color.

The boys smiled wide, cheesy smiles at Pastor Ruhlen.

"Dudes," he continued in his traditional surfer-dude-gone-overboard-style, "when fear gets hold of you, it grabs you like a bullsnake, squeezin' the life outta ya. The only one we should fear is God himself—and fearing him means respecting him as our

King. As our Lord. As the Big Dude we love so much that we don't want to do wrong stuff that would sadden him."

"Let me get this straight," Lamar quietly pressed Matt. "You *brought* Sam the laptop? Yesterday?"

"Why shouldn't I? It was hers to begin with."

"Yeah, but how did you *get* it? You're grounded from it!"

"I . . . borrowed it. My dad said I could use the laptop if it's a matter of life and death, which it is."

"Mmm-hmm."

Matt looked back over his other shoulder. There was Isabel, concentrating on the pastor's message. It even seemed that she was taking notes. How nice life must be for her, without the kind of cares he had—no laptop, no bullies, no wrestling thugs, no craziness.

"It's under my bed," Matt whispered to Lamar.

Lamar's mouth dropped open again.

Gill leaned forward again. "What?" he shouted.

Alfonzo turned. "Shhh!"

Pastor Ruhlen paused again and peered down at the boys. They smiled wide, cheesy smiles at him.

"Now take down these scriptures," he said, continuing his message. Students like Isabel quickly obeyed. "They'll show you how to be 2:52 guys and girls—who can beat fear."

*I need more than scriptures,* Matt thought, *I need strength.*

"The laptop is under your bed?" Lamar asked.

"When I got home, my mom was already there. I didn't have time to put it back in her closet."

Gill leaned forward. "As your manager, I'll take care of your obituary."

A few minutes later, Pastor Ruhlen wrapped up with a "So you see, bros, the Truth will set you free!" Then he picked up his guitar and led the group in one final chorus. Matt couldn't remember the words for anything. He couldn't help but look back at the big guys one more time. *Why,* he wondered, *didn't I take up weight training at age eight?*

As the room emptied, Lamar, Gill, and Alfonzo stood next to Matt, talking, trying to cheer him up.

 Matt stayed seated, feeling more distant by the moment as he realized the end of the night meant the beginning of tomorrow. And tomorrow he would be thrown onto the wrestling mat again, probably with someone twice his size, a piece of meat thrown to the dogs.

Suddenly, Hulk appeared, dropping a heavy hand on Matt's shoulder. Matt buckled under the weight.

"Hey, Calhan," Hulk said. "Ya got my list?"

"It's at home." Matt moved out from under Hulk's hand and stood up. "I'll bring it to school tomorrow."

Hulk pointed to Matt. "Better be good."

"Hey, Hulk!" Gill shouted. "You missed your opportunity, man! My docket is now full. Anything you want to say to Mr. Calahan, you need to run through me first."

Hulk scowled at Gill and lifted a fist.

"But hey!" Gill added, taking a step back. "Who needs formalities? As long as Matt says it's okay, you can just talk directly to him."

Hulk turned around and walked back to his thug-buddies.

"I feel like such a wimp," Matt said to his friends, dropping to his seat.

"You are a wimp," Gill said, dropping into the seat next to him. "We're *all* wimps."

Alfonzo slapped Gill's chest. "Speak for yourself."

Lamar put his hand on Matt's shoulder. "Matt, don't sweat it. Coach says he saw potential in you, remember? You'll do fine in PE tomorrow."

Matt felt his body tense. "Actually, I think I might get sick before then."

"Sick?" Alfonzo repeated.

"Yeah, I'm feeling sick already."

Alfonzo clearly didn't buy it. "You're thinking about quitting, aren't you? You gonna ditch?"

Matt looked at Lamar and Gill. "Well, I'm not as good at wrestling as you, Alfonzo."

"I thought you said we have to live up to a higher standard."

"We do," Lamar agreed.

"Well, isn't ditching the same as lying?"

Matt let out a quick short breath. "Yeah," he whispered, "but the truth is, I'm not as strong as guys like you."

"The chances of you wrestling Hulk again are slim to none," Lamar said. "Coach likes to rotate."

Matt sighed. "Thank God! Otherwise, I'd be dead for sure. But even so—a bunch of those guys are big and strong and athletic—everything I'm not. What am I thinking? I can't make this team! I'm gonna get beat up out there!"

"It's true, my client always gets beat up in P.E.," Gill said.

"Look, do you want to be on the team?" Alfonzo challenged.

"Yes," Matt said not-so-convincingly.

"It's not all about strength," Alfonzo countered. "It's smarts. Isn't that what Coach told you?"

"Yeah," Matt said, "but it's gonna take a *lot* of smarts to make up for their strength."

"Yeah," Gill agreed, "and without the laptop, there's just no way Matt can get that smart that fast. Is there?"

Back home, with his mother downstairs watching TV in the living room, and his father at the hardware store, Matt pulled the laptop out from underneath his bed. He then sneaked down the hall, careful not to make a noise, and lifted it to the top of his parents' closet. As he stretched, the two-day old bruise on his arm ached. He got mad just thinking about going back onto the mat and getting beat up again. Staying *off* the mat was the *smart* thing to do. But he *did* want to make the team. Still, Gill was right: There was no way he could get smart enough fast enough to beat the other guys' strength.

Then Matt froze.

He felt the weight of the laptop in his hands.

Matt looked behind him. The hallway was empty. Canned laughter rose from the television downstairs. For a long, hard moment, he listened for any sound of movement in the house. Nothing.

Matt peered at the laptop. There was *one* way he could get that smart that fast . . .

As quick as he could, Matt pulled the laptop back down, popped open the lid and pressed the power button. He waited and waited for the machine to boot. He listened to the empty hallway intently, for creaks or cracks, but heard only his own heart beating a thousand times per minute. Finally, he launched the word processor that was like no other. Off the top of his head, adrenaline pumping, Matt used all the creativity he could muster to write a quick story:

> Matt Calahan was no ordinary wrestler. No,
> he was an extraordinary wrestler. But was
> it because of his history as a
> professional athlete like no other? No.
> Was it because he was a humongous guy? Um,
> no. Was it his superior strength?
> Obviously not. It was because in the Jr.
> High wrestling world, he was known as "Dr.
> Smart."

Matt furled his brow. Not his most creative stuff, but under the circumstances, it would have to do. He added:

> When Matt "Dr. Smart" Calahan stepped onto
> the mat, he could remember everything he'd
> ever heard about wrestling. The facts and
> moves of wrestling flooded his mind like a
> wild rush of whitewater torrential rains.
> After all, they didn't call him Dr. Smart
> for nothing.

Matt bit his bottom lip. He wasn't exactly sure what all that meant, but it sounded good. Satisfied, Matt smiled. He pressed the key with the clock face on it. On screen, the cursor flashed white-to-gold and back, turning into a clock, ticking forward with fury.

When it finished, Matt shut the computer down and quickly stuffed it back into his parents' closet, under the shoebox. And this time he barely noticed the pain in his arm. *After all,* he thought, *what could possibly go wrong?*

## 4

# Not So Smart

Oooo!" the boys in the gym class shouted, wincing at the sight of one of their own getting smashed under the weight of another.

"That's gonna leave a mark," Alfonzo said to Matt and Lamar.

The three boys were sitting with their class watching the match.

Lamar nudged Alfonzo and Alfonzo looked at Matt. "Ah, but it's not so bad," Alfonzo said.

Matt looked at Alfonzo as if to ask, "What are you, nuts?" But then he assured Alfonzo, telling him truthfully, "It's no big deal, really. I'm ready for today."

"You are?" Lamar asked.

Matt nodded. *More than you know.* All morning, as he had moved from one class to another, he actually found himself eagerly anticipating his match. He had seen the laptop work wonders in the past and he was ready to see it go to work again. Still, in the back of his mind, guilt niggled at him for using the laptop in the first place, let alone taking it out of his parents' closet. Nonetheless, that feeling aside, Matt was eager to turn his wrestling worries around once and for all.

*Smack! Pop!* The larger boy pinned the smaller to the mat and held him down mercilessly.

From across the gym, Coach Plymouth blew his whistle, ending the match. The coach had jogged into the room from the bathroom, where he had disappeared *again*.

"Good match, boys!" The coach walked over to his clipboard and scribbled something on it as the boys exited the mat. "Okay," he said after a moment, "let's do . . . Hulk Hooligan and Marty Lawrence on the far mat, and on this mat . . . Phillip Grove and Matt Calahan."

Matt felt his heart beating faster.

"Phillip Grove," Lamar said. "You can beat him."

"Yeah," Alfonzo agreed. "Don't worry about the fact that he was the quarterback—"

"I'm not worried," Matt said, wiping his hands with his towel and throwing it on top of his gym bag.

"You're not?" Lamar asked.

"No. I'll do fine. Trust me. Gill will be proud to be my manager once this match is done."

Matt jumped forward and stepped onto the mat. Just as he had typed in the laptop, the second his foot touched, it was like a moment of deep revelation. Everything he ever remembered being taught about wrestling rushed into his mind. *Two points for take-downs and reversals. Penalty calls include stalling, illegal holds, and unsportsmanlike conduct. Leaving the mat is a technical violation.* Matt shook his head. He jogged to the center of the mat.

He looked at Phillip Grove as Coach Plymouth joined them. He shook each of their hands, called for a clean match, and then Matt and Phillip shook hands. Coach blew his whistle.

The match began.

"Umph!"

Phillip slammed into Matt's chest, then his arms flew around Matt and tightened.

Matt stepped backward, then forward. He tried to gain hold of Phillip without losing his stance, but he couldn't focus.

"Folkstyle wrestling is also known as scholastic or collegiate wrestling!" Matt cheered. "Points are awarded for pinning or escaping from an opponent!"

"I know!" Phillip shouted.

Phillip threw his weight forward and he and Matt hit the ground. He nearly got the advantage, but Matt flipped over, on top of Phillip. Phillip rolled sideways, breaking out from the bottom position, and came out on top of Matt, gaining control.

"Reversal!" Coach Plymouth shouted. "Two points for Phillip."

Matt tried concentrating harder. "A reversal is when the wrestler in the underneath, defensive position comes from the bottom and gains control while in-bounds!"

Phillip looked at Matt, who was struggling to keep his shoulder blades from becoming parallel to the mat. "What are you? Dr. Smart?" he asked.

"Well, I'm not Dan Gable who had a record of 182–1 in his college and prep matches!" Matt felt his grip loosen as facts and rules and trivial pursuits flooded his mind, suddenly making him squeeze his eyes tightly in concentration. He just couldn't think about anything else . . . including what he was doing!

Taking advantage of the moment, Phillip pressed Matt's shoulders flat on the mat, pinning him for two seconds. Coach blew his whistle and Phillip jumped up, triumphant. Coach threw Phillip's hand in the air.

"Winner!" Coach shouted. "Okay, that was long enough. Good match, boys."

Matt shook his head, trying to shake loose all the overwhelming information. "A singlet is a one-piece uniform that wrestlers wear!" he shouted.

Alfonzo stepped in and grabbed Matt's hand, pulling him up. He and Lamar rushed him off the mat. Once they did, Matt felt his head clear like the sun emerging from behind thick, dark clouds.

"What happened?" Alfonzo asked.

"I . . . I'm Dr. Smart," Matt said, shaking the cobwebs out of his head. "Anyone have an aspirin?"

Lamar looked at Matt suspiciously.

On the other mat, Hulk brought down his opponent with a thud.

*Ka-bam!* Matt's locker door slammed shut in front of him like a bear trap. Matt barely pulled his fingers out in time. On the other side of the crashing door, Hulk Hooligan guffawed. "Yer so funny, Calhan! Ya should see yer face!"

"Cal-*a*-han," Matt corrected the caveman-esqe bully. "And I'm not in the mood. I've got a headache."

"Me too," the big lug said, "and I'm lookin' at him right now. Haw-haw!"

Matt rolled his eyes.

"So where's my list?" Hulk asked in a quieter voice than usual.

"Please?" Matt reminded him.

Hulk put a fist in front of Matt's face.

"Close enough." Matt placed his fingers on the latch to his locker and Hulk put a meaty hand on the door, holding it shut.

"It's inside," Matt said.

Hulk released his hand. "So," he taunted as Matt retrieved the list, "ya get yer other arm bruised today?"

Matt didn't want to answer because, well, he *did*. "I guess I'm not as strong as Alfonzo," he admitted, "or as ... *thick* ... as you."

"Yuk-yuk-yuk," Hulk mocked. "Ya wanna know da truth?"

"The truth?" Matt repeated, still searching for the list.

"Da truth is bein' strong ain't got nuthin' to do with it."

"Those English lessons didn't take, did they?"

"It's about bein' *scared,* Calhan. Yer scared da second ya step foot in da ring. Dat's why I won da other day. Dat's why I'll *always* win."

Matt finally found the list in between the pages of his science book. He turned to Hulk. "What? You're telling me you're never scared when you step onto the mat—even when you face someone bigger than you?"

"First of all, no one's bigger dan me. Second, no. No fear. I know I gotcha beat."

"You just know it?" Matt asked, fishing. "Mind over matter—is that what you mean?"

Hulk blew Matt's question off, snatching the list out of his hand. "Whatever."

Matt waited while Hulk read the list of nutritional foods to himself.

A few moments later, Hulk said, "Ya want me to eat dis stuff? Celery with peanut butter? Low-fat yogurt? Wheat bread?"

"That's what you asked for," Matt said. "Follow that list and do sit-ups and pushups every day, and it'll help."

"I'd better—within da week."

"I'm not a miracle worker," Matt argued. "It'll take time."

"I give it da week," Hulk repeated. "And if it don't work fast enough, ya know what I'm gonna do?"

Matt gulped. "You're gonna beat the snot outta me?"

Hulk smiled. "Yup. Yer gonna find bruises in places ya didn't even know ya had."

When Matt got home from school, he looked around, and with the coast clear, he retrieved the front door key from the little, magnetic black box in the drainpipe at the corner of his house. He opened his front door and returned it to its spot. Without missing a beat, Matt rushed upstairs, slid the laptop out from under the shoebox and pulled it down. He flipped the lid open and powered on the machine. As it booted, guilt kicked in and Matt looked over his shoulder. "It's only two minutes," he said to himself, "and it's a matter of life and death. Dad said it was okay if it was a matter of life and death." Still not entirely convinced, Matt repeated, "It's only two minutes." Sitting on the floor, Matt finally started the word processor and typed as fast as he could:

> Okay, so Matt Calahan didn't want to be "Dr. Smart" anymore. He realized it took more than a bunch of facts to win at wrestling. It took beating the system. It took mind over matter.

Even as Matt typed, he scolded himself for thinking that something Hulk said might have some merit to it. Still . . . at this point, he was willing to try anything. He had two bruised arms and he wasn't about to become a fool again in front of his entire class. He continued:

> Yes, when daring Matt Calahan stepped onto the mat, he just knew he could defeat his opponent. He just knew he won—before he even started. This wrestling thing was a piece of cake. Chocolate cake with cherry frosting. This was Matt's day of reckoning.

Matt tapped the floor with his fingers. He wasn't exactly sure what that meant, but it sounded good.

*Oh!* Matt thought. While he was at it . . .

Hulk loves the diet list Matt created for him, and he follows it zealously.

With a smirk, Matt slapped the clock-faced key, causing the on-screen cursor to turn into a clock and flash gold, ticking forward like lightning.

As fast as he could, Matt turned the laptop off and placed it back where it belonged. He put the shoebox on top of it, then retraced his steps out of his parents' bedroom and back to his own. "It was only two minutes," he said to himself one more time. *And finally everything is solved. What could possibly go wrong this time?*

# Upside Down

## 5

Matt Calahan and ... Alfonzo Zarza on deck," Coach Plymouth announced.

Matt and Alfonzo looked at each other, blank-faced.

"Well, let's go," Alfonzo said.

"Go easy on him," Lamar ordered as Alfonzo stood up.

"No!" Matt cried, looking around at some of the other guys in his class. "You don't have to go easy on me. I've got this one won."

"You do?" Lamar asked.

"Of course."

"Okay ..."

Matt and Alfonzo waited until the boys before them were finished, and then they walked to the center of the mat. They shook the coach's hand, shook each other's hands, and then the coach blew his whistle and backed up.

Matt and Alfonzo crouched and circled each other for a few moments, staring into each others' eyes. Then Matt stood up straight.

"What are you doing?" Alfonzo whispered.

"What do you mean? I won, didn't I?"

"Um . . . we haven't started yet. We have to go three minutes."

"But I'm already the winner. Piece of cake. Chocolate cake. Cherry frosting."

"Oh, I get it," Alfonzo said with a smirk. "You're trying to psyche me out. Won't work."

With that, Alfonzo charged forward and threw his arms around Matt, his full weight hitting him, as the two boys crashed to the mat like bricks. Matt didn't even resist. He felt a soft pain roll through his body. He was sure he must have bruised something.

"Two points for Alfonzo," Coach announced, "takedown."

"What are you doing?" Matt grunted through gritted teeth, now pushing back. "I've already won."

A few seconds later, Coach added, "Three points for Alfonzo—near fall."

"Does it look like you're winning?" Alfonzo challenged, struggling to keep his advantage. "You just gave me five points."

Matt pushed and pulled, but he couldn't seem to beat Alfonzo's strength. The guy was just built for sports. Matt tried to slink sideways, but Alfonzo countered the move, trapping Matt's legs and arms with his own. Finally, Matt felt his body go limp and Alfonzo pinned him.

Coach blew his whistle. "Keep going," he ordered.

"But I won," Matt protested.

"Good spirit," Coach Plymouth told him, "but I want action, Matt. I want to see you put what we learned into practice. Now quit stalling or Alfonzo's getting another point."

"But I already won," Matt argued.

"One point, Alfonzo," Coach said, marking his clipboard.

The boys stood up and started circling each other again.

"Ooof!" Alfonzo brought Matt to the ground.

"Takedown! Two points!"

*Bam!* Alfonzo pinned him again.

Coach Plymouth blew his whistle. He didn't even bother announcing the final score. "Okay, thanks, boys." As quickly as it had begun, it ended. Alfonzo jumped up and Coach lifted his arm into the air. "Winner!" he shouted. "By a long shot."

The class clapped, while Matt lay on the mat wondering why; he was still pretty sure *he* was the winner.

The walk home from school was about fifteen minutes. But many times it took longer since Matt, Lamar, Gill, and Alfonzo liked to take it easy after school—especially during this time when Matt was grounded. It was about the *only* time, other than youth group and school itself, that all four boys could spend time together.

The air was crisp and cool, the ground and foliage still brown from cooler months.

Matt couldn't let it go. "I just don't understand it," he said. "I really thought I won."

"I wish I'd have been there." Gill shook his head, as though he had missed the Superbowl. "I *should* have been there. Managers make all the difference, you know."

"You're good, Matt," Alfonzo said to his friend. "I just got the advantage on you."

"Yeah, but it wasn't supposed to happen that way."

"Well, I'm going to keep beating you while I can. 'Cuz when you get your laptop back, I won't have a chance," he said with a smile.

Matt froze in place. Lamar bumped into him. Gill and Alfonzo stopped. They all looked at Matt.

"Um . . . I used the laptop," he told them.

Lamar placed a hand on top of his head. "What?"

"You used the laptop and you still got walloped?!" Gill shouted. "You really *are* bad at wrestling."

"That's why I was sure I won. But for some reason, it didn't work."

"But you're still grounded from the laptop," Alfonzo said, stating the obvious.

Matt just looked at him.

"Matt, what are you thinking?" Lamar asked. "If your parents find out, they could take away the laptop permanently."

"I know, I know."

"I'm serious," Lamar pushed. "You shouldn't disobey 'em." He thought for a moment, then, "What did you type anyway?"

"Just—you know—that I won by mind over matter. I knew going into it that I was better than my opponent was. I heard mind over matter was the key."

"Well, where'd you get an idea like that?" Lamar asked.

"Uh, Hul-Hulk." Matt realized how silly he sounded.

Lamar's face dropped. "Well the reason it didn't work," he said, "is because mind over matter *doesn't* work—ever. It sounds more like pride, anyway. You underestimated your opponent, man."

"I feel so stupid." Matt knew he had let his judgment get clouded, and now that he had admitted the truth, it sounded even more ridiculous than he had originally thought. "It's just ... you know, Coach Plymouth wants me to make the wrestling team ... my parents want me to make the wrestling team ..."

Gill added, "Your manager wants you to make the wrestling team . . ."

"Yeah," Lamar said, "but do *you* want to be on the wrestling team?"

"Yes!" Matt exclaimed. "I do! Why does everyone keep asking me that?"

"Then you know you can't use the laptop—or you'll always wonder if you could have done it yourself."

"I know . . . I just don't have the strength by myself. I'm likely to get hurt before I even get rolling."

Alfonzo threw his schoolbooks on the ground. "Matt, c'mon. Put your stuff down. I'll show you some moves. You won't need the laptop."

"Really?"

"Yeah, c'mon."

Matt nodded and slid his backpack off his shoulders. He dropped it to the ground and looked at Alfonzo. "Okay, what?"

"Try to take me down," Alfonzo said.

Matt looked around the quiet neighborhood. A woman was out raking leaves. A car was pulling out of a driveway. A dog barked. "Here?"

"Do it!"

Matt shrugged. At once, he shot forward, slamming Alfonzo in the chest. But Alfonzo was an immovable rock. He pressed back with even more strength. *Ka-foom! Boom!* With a quick maneuver, Alfonzo flipped Matt around and onto the ground. A split-second later, he had him pinned; Matt couldn't move in any direction.

"You were going easy on me in the ring, weren't you?" Matt asked weakly.

Alfonzo smiled.

"You've got to teach me that move," Matt said.

Alfonzo stood up. He grabbed Matt's hand and helped him to his feet. "Okay, let's do it in slow motion. Come at me."

Matt did. He wrapped his arms around Alfonzo and pushed.

"Okay, wait," Alfonzo said. "See where your weight is?"

Matt stopped moving. "It's against you."

"Right," Alfonzo said. "So a smart player will realize that and shift like this." Suddenly, Alfonzo shifted to the side—not unlike he had done earlier in the ring—and Matt lost his balance. Alfonzo countered by placing his feet on either side of Matt, twisting around and pulling Matt to the ground, underneath him. "And I've got you."

"It's not mind over matter," Matt said, looking up quizzically at Alfonzo. "It's just using my mind."

"The mind God gave you," Lamar added.

"Smarts," Alfonzo said, "and speed. You do that and you'll find that you've even got an advantage on me."

"I doubt that. You're really strong."

"No strength is a match for a good strategy."

Alfonzo stood up again and had Matt reclaim his position before he ran into him. "Okay stop. Now here's where I can use your weight against you. But if you're as fast as you are, you can anticipate that and shift your weight back."

Matt smiled. "And prevent you from taking me down." He shifted his weight back as Alfonzo attempted to take him down. Alfonzo tried twisting Matt around, but Matt thwarted the attempt. Suddenly Alfonzo flipped around the other way and took Matt down face-first.

Matt lay with his face in the grass. "What happened?" he asked.

"I went the other way."

"Right."

Suddenly the ground rumbled. Alfonzo tumbled off Matt and onto the sidewalk. Matt turned his head just in time to see him jump up and rush his attacker— bleached-hair bully, Hulk Hooligan. When he hit Hulk, carrots and celery sticks flew in fifty directions. Matt jumped up and he and Lamar rushed between the two guys shouting, "Whoa! Whoa!"

"The winner gets a free management consultation!" Gill announced.

"Whoa! Whoa!" Matt and Lamar struggled and pushed until they were finally able to part Alfonzo and Hulk.

"Hulk! What are you doing?" Matt cried. "And Alfonzo—turn the other cheek, man! Higher standard, remember?"

Alfonzo's face hardened. "Oh right, just like you live by a higher standard, going against your parents and using your—"

"Stop!" Lamar ordered everyone before Alfonzo could say the word "laptop."

Hulk reached down and picked up a carrot off the sidewalk. He blew it off and chomped down.

Lamar looked Hulk up and down. "Have you lost weight?" he asked. Then he turned to Matt with his eyes wide open. "You *didn't*."

"It was a matter of life and death!" Matt said, defending his decision to use the laptop on Hulk.

"Matt, have you gone crazy?" Lamar asked point-blank.

"My client refuses to answer that," Gill told Lamar.

"What?" Hulk picked a celery stick off an anthill. "I dunno what yer problem is," he said to Lamar. "I was just savin' Matt from dis bully."

"Oh, *I'm* a bully?" Alfonzo challenged Hulk.

"I don't believe this!" Matt shouted at Lamar. "You're yelling at me and . . . *Hulk* comes to my rescue? Is this an episode of the *Twilight Zone*?"

"I'm not yelling at you!" Lamar yelled back. "You're just not acting like yourself!"

"Ya got a spur in yer rear against Calhan?" Hulk prodded Lamar.

"Cal-*a*-han!" Matt snatched his backpack off the ground. "Forget it," he said, storming off. "You guys work it out. I have somewhere I'm supposed to be."

# The Trouble with the Laptop

## 6

Behind the Happy Gas gas station, Matt pulled his laptop out of his gym bag and booted it up. "You know my life is turning upside down?" he asked Sam.

Sam, sitting beside him on the ground with her legs crossed, nodded silently, even sadly. Her coat was open, and her clothing was black underneath. Her hat was sitting upside-down on the pavement beside her, her leather gloves folded inside. It was the first time Matt had seen her appear anything near "relaxed" . . . ironically, at a time Matt was anything *but* relaxed.

"I didn't mean to use the laptop," Matt admitted. "I just did. Not near as much as I have before. Just a little bit. Usually I'm not grounded from it. Anyway, suddenly everything went wrong. My best friends are fighting with me, my enemy is helping me. And I . . . I don't know why I'm telling you this. Sorry."

Sam's lips upturned. "You have to use your best judgment, Matt. That's all you can do. So long as you use the laptop for the greater good, it's okay."

Matt found himself agreeing with that statement less and less. He didn't think it was his judgment to make—especially when he was going against his parents' wishes. He watched the Wordtronix logo spin around on the laptop screen. "I know. You said that before. You said it was all right to use the laptop so long as no one gets hurt. Well . . . it may be a matter of life and death . . . but I think *I'm* getting hurt."

 Matt turned his head and looked straight into Sam's hazel eyes. She looked back into his own eyes, an unspoken understanding that no other two people in the world could have had.

Sam's lips parted, then closed again. She fixed her eyes on the laptop. "I had no idea it could gain such a hold on some people. It seemed so *right* . . . but suddenly, it grasps you and won't let go." Then she solemnly added, "You feel like you can't live without it."

Matt couldn't take his eyes off her.

"Until you're forced to," Sam continued. "Then you realize what it has done to you . . . to others."

Matt's mood suddenly changed. "I'm not going to let it get hold of me like that," he said boldly.

Sam smiled weakly. "I know. I believe that." Then, "All this you're facing now . . . it's growing pains. What makes you different is that you're determined to do what's right. That's why it picked you as its owner."

"I don't think it was the laptop that picked me," Matt said softly. Still, he had wondered many times if he had been *chosen* to have it. But then the questions would surface: Would God do that? And if so, why? Was there something he was supposed to do with the laptop? Some reason he should have it instead of someone else? "I don't know. But I *am* determined to do my best with it. To make the right choices." Matt huffed. "I just made the wrong ones this time."

"It's not always easy to make the right choices," Sam admitted, "but it's much easier when you have a heart that wants to do right. You've got that. I've known people who don't."

"So why won't *you* use the laptop anymore?"

Sam looked into the sky. "It ruined my life, Matt. Well, others ruined my life with it. I don't want a thing to do with it."

Matt chuckled. "So you stick *me* with it."

"I *trust* you with it," Sam corrected. "You keep it out of the wrong hands."

Matt appreciated her blind trust in his strength of character . . . but he was sure having a hard time *not* misusing the laptop right now. "So how can I get rid of this . . . fear . . . without relying on the laptop?"

"I don't know the answer to that," Sam admitted. "But I do know this: In the right hands, the laptop can do a world of good. But in the wrong hands, it brings the world to ruins. We must stop those who could use it for wrong. Lives depend on it, Matt."

The laptop was fully booted and Matt turned the screen for Sam to see. "Okay, show me what to do."

"The CD is in the drive?"

Matt nodded.

"All right then, open the picture file you found on it."

Matt's finger slid over the small, square touchpad and the cursor on the screen zipped around. He opened the CD folder and selected the lone picture file. It looked just like it had before: a big, muddied picture of gray and black boxes. He figured it was a satellite photo of some kind. In one section, there appeared to be a sign on a building—maybe a logo. But Matt was only guessing.

"Press F11," Sam ordered.

Matt did. The image became sharper.

"Now, holding down shift, press the right arrow three times."

Matt did. The image rotated and sharpened again, like a painting taking shape. Matt squinted.

"F11 again."

Matt pressed F11 again. Like magic, the image popped into place. His eyes grew wide. The muddied gray splotch of a picture had changed to a crisp drawing of boxes and lines. The part he thought was a sign was a legend. He frowned as he turned to Sam.

"It's a blueprint," Matt said.

"This isn't just *any* blueprint," Sam replied. "This is *the* blueprint."

"To what?"

"The Facilities."

Matt's eyes flickered to the blueprint and then back to Sam. "I'm not following."

"This is where the laptop was born, Matt." Sam pointed to a square in the middle. "In this room. I believe the complete records to the laptop's construction are still here."

Matt swallowed hard. "So you want to get them?"

"I want to destroy them."

"So how are you going to do that?"

"I've got the blueprint. I can walk right in."

Matt wasn't sure he understood any of this. He noticed small triangles with corresponding numbers at the end of each thin hallway. They weren't listed in the legend. "What are these?" he asked, pointing to a triangle.

"Cameras."

"Your enemy."

Sam smiled. "My asset."

"So you want to destroy the records so . . ."

"So this madness can come to an end," Sam said. "They don't know where the laptop is. That's for certain. And if we can destroy these records, we can stop them from ever creating something like it again."

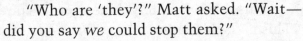

"Who are 'they'?" Matt asked. "Wait— did you say *we* could stop them?"

Sam stood up. "Enough for now. I'll let you know more when the time is right."

Matt set the laptop down and stood beside Sam. "You know you're a very mysterious person?"

"All secrets are revealed in time." Sam buttoned up her coat, placed her hat on her head, pulling her hair up underneath it, and slid her hands into her thin, black gloves. She turned and walked away. But just before rounding the corner, she stopped and turned back to Matt.

"What?" Matt asked.

"You're not afraid of me anymore, are you?"

Matt scrunched his nose. "Not really," he said truthfully. "Though . . . I'm not sure why."

"One night when I was young," Sam said, "I saw a monster in my room. I couldn't sleep all night. It just stared at me from over in the corner. A dark, thin monster. Finally, in the morning, the sun brightened

my room and I realized there was no monster there . . .
only my coat, lying awkwardly on top of my stereo. I
had put it there the night before." She paused and then
added, "Maybe you're no longer scared of me because
you know the truth now—about who I am."

Matt heard Pastor Ruhlen's words echo in his
mind. "The truth will set you free."

"Maybe," Matt whispered.

And Sam departed.

Matt smiled. He sat down and picked up the laptop to turn it off. But before he did, he opened the
word processor and typed:

> Hulk no longer loves his diet just because
> he has to. He can feel about it however he
> wants. And Matt no longer tries to use
> mind over matter or be Dr. Smart. He just
> be's the person God made him to be.

*Be's? Oh well, it works.* He figured if nothing else,
this could help make things right again. Sure, he might
get bruises in P.E., but at least he would get them trying to be noble, instead of with a feeling of guilt. As he
pressed the clock-faced key, he prayed that God would
give him wisdom and show him how to have strength.

Matt looked at his watch. Four forty-five. His
parents would be home soon—and he had to get the

laptop back. As Matt stuffed it into his gym bag, he wondered if he should confess to his parents that he had hijacked the laptop not once, but twice. It would be, after all, the right thing to do. But Matt felt his stomach turn at the thought. According to Sam it was a matter of life and death. For the greater good. So he was justified. Right? And he had negated his own stories . . . so that cleared that up, Matt convinced himself. For now, he just needed to get the laptop back where it belonged. Confession would be something he could do later . . . maybe *much* later.

Matt biked home speedily, his gym bag on his handlebars. He exited Oleander Street and slid into his driveway. He jumped off and was about to retrieve his key from the hidden box in the drainpipe when he heard a voice from across the street. It sounded like newly-spun honey calling his name.

Matt whirled around like an Ice Capades hopeful and saw Alfonzo's sister, Isabel Zarza, standing beside her mailbox. He was pretty sure, as often as he saw her there, it was no longer just a coincidence. He grinned as she waved to him, her fingers toppling one after another. He held his gym bag in one hand, raising the other hand to wave back.

*Crash!* And his bike toppled to the ground. Matt jumped. Whoops—with all the excitement, he had forgotten to use the kickstand. Isabel giggled at his antics and he tried to act like he had purposely made his bike fall over. He threw his gym bag over his shoulder like a tennis pro throwing a towel over his shoulder after a match. Inside the bag, his laptop smacked him in the back, knocking him forward. Isabel giggled again.

Matt made his way down the driveway and crossed the street.

"Hey," he said. "What's up?"

"Just getting my mail." Isabel held up a stack of letters.

"Hey, look at that," Matt said, pointing to the stack. "You got another letter to Mr. Occupant. I thought he moved out."

Isabel gave Matt a puzzled stare.

Matt brushed it off. "One of Gill's jokes," he said apologetically.

Matt and Isabel looked at each other for a short moment. Isabel's long, black hair that flowed down her back like a waterfall was pulled straight back in a ponytail. She wore black jeans and a thick, blue sweater. Matt heard a car. He quickly turned. False alarm; it wasn't his mom.

"Sorry, but I'm kinda rushed today," Matt said. "I have . . . some things to take care of before my mom gets home."

Isabel smiled.

Matt turned.

"Wait."

Matt turned back.

Isabel smiled again. "I . . . um . . . I mean, Alfonzo told me about what you said about how we need to live up to a higher standard, you know, since we're Christians now. You know, no lying, stuff like that."

Matt nodded, the laptop poking him in the small of his back.

"Well, I didn't really come out here to get the mail."

Matt searched Isabel's deep brown eyes. He gulped. "You didn't?"

"No . . . I . . ." Then she quickly said, "You're going to think it's stupid."

"Oh, no," Matt assured her. "No. What?"

Isabel grit her teeth. "You promise?"

Matt heard another car. He turned. Another false alarm. He really had to get the laptop back. "Really, I promise."

"Okay." Isabel pulled out a piece of notebook paper, folded twice, from underneath the pile of letters. She handed it to Matt without saying a word. He took it, but didn't open it.

"What's this?"

"Well, I know you've been having trouble in wrestling. Alfonzo told me."

Matt narrowed his eyes. *Thanks, Alfonzo.*

"I know you want to make the team. Well, Pastor Ruhlen gave us some scriptures the other night in youth group. Remember? About not having fear? I know you won't let fear stop you, but just in case things get rough, I thought these might help. I looked some others up and added to it. Didn't take too long."

Matt wasn't quite sure if he should thank her or feel totally embarrassed. He opted for a mix of the two. "Er . . . thanks . . . I guess."

Another car drove by. Matt couldn't remember when the street had been so busy.

"You don't have to read it now," Isabel said. "No pressure."

Thankful for the release, he slung his gym bag forward and slid the paper inside. "Cool. I appreciate it. I'll check it out later."

Isabel looked at the ground. "I didn't mean to embarrass you," she told him. "I'm sorry."

"No!" Matt exclaimed. "Really—it's very cool. I think my mind's just on other things: making the team, staying alive, higher standards. Usual stuff. But really, thank you."

Isabel nodded awkwardly. Matt quickly dismissed himself, sure he was about to get caught any moment. He felt like such a heel, like he wasn't giving Isabel the time she deserved, or thanking her like he should for breaking out of her comfort zone to create a note of encouragement for him. But he also knew he valued his life. Leaving the moment between them more awkward than he had since he first met Isabel, they parted company.

Matt retrieved the key from the drainpipe, then turned to give Isabel one last good-bye wave, but she had already gone inside.

## 7

# The Snap Heard Around the Gym

Yer *so* gonna pay, Calhan," Hulk threatened Matt, a Snickers, a Butterfinger, and a Three Musketeers in his fist.

The milk chocolate coating on Hulk's teeth made Matt's eyes cross. In an attempt to keep his school lunch down, Matt turned away from the bully. "Where's Coach?" he asked Lamar, sitting beside him in the gym with the rest of his class.

Lamar shrugged. "I think he's going to the bathroom again."

"What's the deal?" Matt asked. "Does he have a bladder problem or something?"

"No," Alfonzo said, "he's on some kinda new diet. He has to drink twenty glasses of water a day."

Matt's eyes popped. "Twenty glasses?! I hope it works."

"Oh, it should," Alfonzo said, nodding. "It came from one of those grocery-stand newspapers."

"Like *you* know," Hulk taunted Alfonzo.

Alfonzo opened his mouth to say something.

"Higher standards," Lamar reminded him.

Alfonzo closed his mouth.

"Why didn't ya tell *me* about dat diet, Calhan?" Hulk interjected. "Maybe I'd be in shape by now!"

Matt turned back to Hulk. "What happened to the carrots and celery?"

Hulk threw his shoulders back. "I don't know *how* ya got me ta eat dose. I hate dat stuff." He finished off his candy bars, biting all three at once.

Shortly, the double doors burst open, and Coach Plymouth ran into the room. His whistle filled the gym and the boys quickly stopped talking.

"Sorry 'bout that," the coach apologized. "Okay, let me see who's going to wrestle first today . . ." He studied his clipboard.

Matt felt his stomach squirm. Without the laptop's help, he couldn't *imagine* what would happen to him. His healing arms were already starting to ache. But he had made a decision not to be scared. No matter what. Even if he was thrown into the ring with Alfonzo. Or even Hulk. Matt's eyes darted around the gym. Or pretty much anyone. He placed a hand on his stomach and tried to think of what his final words to mankind would be. He really thought his fear would go away once he had made the decision. But it hadn't.

"Oh, this should be a good one," Coach Plymouth continued, marking his clipboard. "Hulk and Alfonzo. On the mat!"

Matt and Lamar's heads snapped to Alfonzo.

"Yeah, this should be good," their friend said with a wink. He stood up and approached the mat.

Matt nudged Lamar. "Hulk and Alfonzo? Hulk has no idea what he's about to face. You should see how strong Alfonzo is. When we wrestled the other day, he was *totally* in control."

"And Hulk wasn't that tough?" Lamar asked Matt.

"Well, Hulk never really used his strength on me," Matt admitted, "so I'm not sure. He was going through that WWE phase, remember?"

Lamar nodded, thoughtfully. "Well, check it out. When Alfonzo beats Hulk, you'll see: You don't need your laptop to help you through this. You just need to use your head."

"I know," Matt said without thinking.

Earlier, Matt had apologized for blowing up at Lamar, Gill, and Alfonzo on the way home from school. Lamar said it was no big deal; they knew Matt was under pressure. Still, Lamar didn't mind throwing in a little anti-laptop word now and then. Matt knew Lamar meant well . . . but Matt had made up his mind about making the team—and staying alive—without the laptop. And he was sticking to it. The laptop was back in his parents' closet where it belonged ... at least until he was no longer grounded.

Alfonzo stood center-mat, opposite Hulk. They shook hands. They shook Coach Plymouth's hand.

"Ya have any last words?" Hulk pressed Alfonzo, his eyes narrowed.

"No, amigo," Alfonzo shot back. "Do you?"

"Just this," Hulk said. And he passed gas.

"Ugh!" Alfonzo shouted, waving his hand in front of his nose.

Hulk laughed as the rest of the class roared and shouted comments like "Disgusting!" and "Gross!" and "Do it again!"

Coach Plymouth, who couldn't hide the sourness on his face, blew his whistle and quieted the class down. "This is an odor-free zone, Hooligan," he said to Hulk, who nodded acknowledgement.

"Unfair tactic," Alfonzo said, pushing away the stale air.

A moment later, the coach stepped to the side of the mat and blew his whistle. Matt watched, wide-eyed, as Alfonzo and Hulk hit each other with full force. They pushed each other for a good twenty seconds, but Hulk's weight gave him the advantage and Alfonzo was soon knocked to the ground. Coach marked two points for Hulk on his clipboard. Matt felt fidgety.

But Alfonzo didn't scare easy. As Hulk dropped to his knees to try to pin Alfonzo to the mat, Alfonzo used his weight against him and rolled Hulk over with a reversal. Two points for Alfonzo. Hulk tried to turn to the side, pressing the mat hard with his feet. The veins in Alfonzo's biceps bulged as he pushed Hulk back, turning his shoulders toward the mat. Matt saw Coach mark another point for Alfonzo, this time for exposure.

"Told ya he's strong," Matt said to Lamar. "Snickers-breath is no match."

Continuing the match, Alfonzo pulled his legs up, attempting to put Hulk in a front headlock with his knees. Hulk anticipated the move and jerked his body up, knocking Alfonzo to the side. Alfonzo came back at him before he had a chance to stand. Hulk's meaty arm wrapped around Alfonzo's neck. He used his weight to turn him over. Hulk got a point for exposure. Three up. It was going to be close.

Matt bit his fingernail. Alfonzo *had* to win. Matt had never seen anyone stronger than Alfonzo. Not even Hulk.

Hulk pushed down. Alfonzo pushed back. Alfonzo's shoulder came down . . . down . . . closer to the mat. He pushed back with all his might. Hulk winced. His teeth gritted like he was squeezing the last bit of juice out of an orange.

Suddenly, Alfonzo ducked his head and threw his right arm around one of Hulk's legs and pulled. The two boys struggled to get the advantage, the last point. Alfonzo nearly threw Hulk back when suddenly, with a determined look on his face, Hulk threw his shoulder on the center of Alfonzo's left forearm and smashed down with all his weight.

*CA-RACKKKK!!* echoed off the gym walls. Everyone in the room gasped as Alfonzo cried out in pain. Hulk rolled and pinned Alfonzo down easily. Coach blew his whistle. Hulk stood up, sweating like a pig, a snarl on his face.

Matt found himself unmovable as he stared at Alfonzo. "Alfonzo?" he whispered.

"Get up, show-off," Hulk said to Alfonzo.

But Alfonzo turned and pressed his face to the mat. "It hurts! It hurts!" he cried, holding his left forearm with his right hand, his knees buckling to his chest.

Matt, along with a few others, stood up to help his friend, but Coach Plymouth ordered the class back and immediately rushed over to Alfonzo.

"He'll be all right," Lamar assured Matt, sounding rather unsure.

Alfonzo fought it back as long as he could, then he started crying, tears mingling with sweat as he kicked his heel against the mat.

Coach Plymouth touched Alfonzo's arm and Matt watched as it began to darken in color right before his eyes. The coach ordered a student to rush to the school nurse's office, while Hulk headed off to the locker room, boasting about an easy match. Matt fought back anger; he had never so wanted to have his laptop with him than he did right then.

The school nurse patched Alfonzo up quickly, temporarily, until his father arrived to take him to the hospital. When the nurse left the room, Alfonzo sniffed, obviously fighting back the throbbing pain. Sitting beside him, Matt couldn't help but stare at his arm. It was taped up now, but he could tell Alfonzo was mustering everything within him to push back the sting.

Matt just couldn't get the sound of the snap out of his head. Gill was there with Matt and Lamar now; he came the moment he heard Alfonzo had broken his arm. "If you need a manager," he'd said, "I'm sure Matt will allow me hiatus to help you."

Alfonzo had thanked him for the offer, but gracefully declined.

"I just can't believe he broke your arm," Matt said for the third time, sounding like a robot programmed with one phrase.

"I don't think he did it on purpose," Lamar defended.

"I believe he did," Alfonzo replied. "I was about to win."

"There's no hope for anyone who wrestles Hulk," Matt said. "He's just. . .I can't believe he broke your arm."

"When you get your laptop back," Alfonzo said, "I want to wrestle him again."

Lamar shook his head.

"At least it's not your good arm," Gill added. "You can still write."

"I'm left-handed," Alfonzo said.

"Oh ... well ... you're sunk then. Sorry."

"Thanks a lot."

Coach Plymouth entered the room again, Hulk behind him. They walked up to Alfonzo and Coach kneeled, placing himself just below eye-level. "You all right, trooper?"

"He broke his arm," Matt said, still stunned, still hearing the echo of the snap off the walls.

"Yeah, ya should be careful," Hulk said.

Coach just stared at Hulk for a long moment, then glanced back at Alfonzo.

Alfonzo nodded. "I won't be able to try out for the team now, will I?"

"Don't worry about that right now," Coach said. "Although..." He pulled his clipboard out from under his arm, flipped forward three pages and moaned. "Oh boy, oh boy. Oh I hadn't anticipated this."

"What?" Lamar wanted to know.

"This throws off our try-outs," Coach Plymouth stated, seeming saddened at the thought. "I was going to have Alfonzo wrestle Jimmy and then Jimmy wrestle Thad and on and on and . . . well, it's just going to take some reworking. And now I have ten reports to fill out before I can get to it."

"Hey, Coach, I'll do it," Hulk offered. "It's da least I could do. After all,"—his eyes darted to Matt—"I owe ya one."

"No!" Matt shouted, jumping up. "I don't think that's a good idea. *I'll* do it!"

Coach Plymouth's eyebrows popped up. "No, Matt, thank you, but I think Hulk is right—he needs to clear his conscience."

"Dat's right," Hulk said with a confident smile.

Matt stared in disbelief as Coach Plymouth pulled out his roster and surrendered it to Hulk. Hulk grabbed it like he was grabbing a Snickers bar and stomped off. Alfonzo assured Coach Plymouth that he would be fine and Coach returned to his office.

Matt gulped. "Hulk's gonna change the roster. He's gonna make it so *I* have to wrestle *him* to make the team."

"This will be your moment of victory!" Gill said happily.

"I am *so* dead."

"You'll be fine," Lamar assured his friend.

"Just use the moves I taught you," Alfonzo said to Matt.

Matt's face dropped. "Um, no offense, but . . . I don't want a broken arm. And I'm not nearly as strong as you are. Besides, Hulk is determined to beat the snot outta me—remember?"

"So what are you going to do?" Gill asked.

 "The only thing I can do," Matt answered.

"You can't use the laptop," Alfonzo pressed Matt. "We live at a higher standard, right?"

"But look at you!" Matt cried. "And we've used it before! To help people!"

"But you weren't *grounded* from it before," Alfonzo reminded him.

Matt muttered, "I am *so* dead."

Matt could barely move. He looked in the mirror and gasped. He was tied up, head to toe, in surgical tape. He looked like a mummy. The only part of his body showing through the cast was a tuft of his black hair, sticking straight up from the top of his head.

*Ka-boom! Ka-boom!*

*The ground shook.*

*Hulk Hooligan trounced into the room like a Franken-gorilla. "Hey Calhan!" he shouted, dressed like a sumo wrestler. "I am Sumo Hulk! No one messes with da Sumo Hulk! I come to finish ya off!"*

*"There's nothing left to finish off!" Matt cried.*

*"Oh yeah dere is!" Hulk bolstered. He reached up and grabbed the tuft of Matt's hair.*

*"No! Not the tuft of my hair!"*

*Hulk guffawed, and put Matt in a headlock.*

*"Nooooo!!!"*

*Hulk grabbed Matt's hair with a meaty fist and ... RI-I-I-I-P ... tore it out of his head.*

"Ugh!" Matt sat straight up in bed, sweat clinging to his face. He felt the top of his head. All his hair was still there. He let out a long breath. It was going to be a long night.

# The Final Bout

## 8

As Matt passed through the kitchen, his hair still wet, his dad stopped him in his tracks.

"On your way to school, Matt?" he asked from behind his newspaper.

Matt's mom, waiting for her toast to pop, smiled at him.

Matt kept moving. The garage door was only a few steps away. He'd have left out the front door, but he *always* left for school out the garage door. He didn't want to raise suspicion.

Sitting at the table, Mr. Calahan put down his newspaper. "Whoa! Whoa there!"

Matt gulped, freezing in place. His gym bag was a bit fatter than usual. Would they notice? He hadn't *wanted* to do it . . . but after being up half the night worrying about his life, he felt he would better be safe than sorry. Even if it did mean doing the wrong thing. The past two times, Sam instructed Matt to steal the laptop *for the greater good.* This time, Matt took it solely for his *own* greater good . . . for the greater good of keeping his body parts intact, to be exact. He didn't want to, but he figured he had to. Wrestling was risky . . . and Matt felt like, without the blessing of great strength, he didn't have a chance.

Matt's stomach tightened and his mouth dried up. He slowly turned to his dad.

"I know what you're going to say," Matt anticipated.

"What am I going to say?" Mr. Calahan asked.

"That I shouldn't do this."

Mr. Calahan smiled. "Just the opposite."

"Huh?"

"I think what you're doing is just fine."

Matt's head tilted. "You do?"

"Yes," Mrs. Calahan agreed. "We're very proud of you for taking such initiative."

Matt squinted. "I'm dreaming again, aren't I?" He pinched himself in the arm. A little pain shot to his elbow. Nope, he wasn't dreaming. *Maybe*, Matt thought, *I woke up in an alternate dimension.*

Mr. Calahan chuckled. He tapped his toast on the side of his plate, knocking off the crumbs. "I just wish we could be there today to *see* you wrestle."

Matt blinked. "Right! Wrestling! You're talking about wrestling! You're glad I'm taking the initiative to *wrestle!*"

Matt's parents looked at each other.

"What did you think we were talking about, honey?" Matt's mom asked.

"Wrestling," Matt quickly snapped back. An awkward silence filled the room for a split second, then he blurted out, "Okay, I'm going to school. Bye!" He grabbed the doorknob to the garage door.

"Don't you want breakfast?" Mrs. Calahan asked.

"No, thanks," Matt said, slipping through the doorway. "My stomach's kinda queasy today. I think I'll pass."

As Matt closed the door, his dad called out, "Do well, Ace!"

Inside the garage, Matt leaned against the doorframe. *Why*, he wondered, *do I have a feeling this is all going to come crashing down on me?*

When Matt entered the gym for P.E. class, and the final tryouts for the wrestling team, he nearly ran into Gill.

"What are you doing here?" Matt asked his friend.

"I am your *manager!*" Gill said, obviously offended. "I am here as your support. Your one-man cheerleader." Gill threw an arm around Matt's shoulder. "If there's anything you need, you just ask Gill-da-man and I'll get it for you. Anything at all."

"Get me out of this," Matt requested.

"Except that," Gill replied. "It's too late. I checked the roll. You're up against Hulk, just like you thought."

Matt wasn't surprised. "He's going to kill me, isn't he?"

"Let's just say I have the number to the school nurse's beeper."

"Thanks for your support, Gill."

Cheesy smile. "What are friends for?"

Gill led Matt to where Lamar and Alfonzo were already sitting.

Matt greeted his friends, then said, "Have you guys all seen the roster? Is it true?"

"It's true," Alfonzo said. "You're up against Hulk." He handed Matt a marker. "Here, sign my cast!"

Matt looked down. The pale blue cast stared back at him. He swallowed hard. "Does it hurt?"

"You know that time I rollerbladed into the cement wall?"

"Yeah."

"Compared to this, that felt good."

Matt popped the tip off the marker and tried to write his name on Alfonzo's cast, but he couldn't hold his hand steady. He pressed down, wrote, and then put the cap back on the pen.

Alfonzo, Lamar, and Gill leaned in to see what Matt had written.

"Slug fondue?" Gill asked.

"No, I think it says 'Scooby Dooey,'" Lamar corrected.

"It says 'Stay strong'," Matt informed his friends.

"Oh right, right," they all said in unison.

Matt handed the marker back to Alfonzo. He saw Hulk enter from the other side of the room. He looked bigger than usual, heavier than usual, meaner than usual.

"I think I need to go . . . somewhere else." Matt started to get up.

"Hey," Alfonzo said, grabbing Matt's arm. "If I can live through this, you can, too."

Matt looked down at Alfonzo's cast again and envisioned Hulk ripping him apart limb by limb.

Hulk caught Matt's eye from across the room. He pointed to him and mouthed, "Yer dead."

Matt's eyes narrowed. He felt a surge of confidence as he placed a hand on his gym bag. "I'll be right back," he told his friends, standing up.

At once, Coach Plymouth's whistle echoed through the gym. "Have a seat, boys," he suggested to Matt and several others who were standing up. "We're getting started now."

Matt felt the surge of confidence evaporate.

"No," Matt said to his friends. "We can't start yet! He's early!"

"It's better to get it over with," Lamar assured Matt. "You'll do fine."

"Yeah, Matt," Gill exclaimed, "it'll be over in seconds!"

"You're not helping," Matt said flatly.

Hulk was already on the mat. He pointed to Matt and then pointed to the ground.

Matt held his hands out in front of himself, open-palmed. "What?"

Gill cleared his throat. "Um, I forgot to tell you."

Matt's eyes darted to Gill. "Forgot to tell me what?"

"You're first."

"You guys, I can't!" Matt gripped his gym bag so tight that his knuckles turned white.

"You'll do fine," Lamar encouraged. "Just keep him busy for three minutes."

"Yeah, right!" Matt shot back. "In three minutes he'll have me in three pieces!"

"Hulk! Matt!" Coach Plymouth called. "On the mat!"

Matt looked around him. All the other guys in his gym class were staring at him now. Matt squeezed the bridge of his nose with his finger and thumb. *Why didn't I write something in the laptop before I came out here? Oh yeah—because if I had, but I* hadn't *been on the list against Hulk, it might have put me up against Hulk anyway.* It was a risk Matt took. It was a bet Matt lost.

No time to think now. Matt released his gym bag. He stood up and popped his lips. "Here goes nothing," he said to no one in particular as he took a step forward.

"Break a leg!" Gill shouted.

The class laughed.

Matt groaned.

As Matt passed the coach, he wanted to ask, "Is this really fair? Is this really right? Do you have insurance to cover this?" But he didn't. He had been roughed up enough in dodge ball to realize P.E. wasn't always fair.

In the center of the mat, Coach Plymouth looked the boys over. He shook each of their hands. He had them shake hands. Hulk squeezed Matt's hand with a death grip. Matt clenched his teeth and took it. And then the coach stepped to the side.

"Ready to get the snot beat outta ya?" Hulk asked.

The coach blew his whistle, starting the match.

With full force, Hulk lunged forward at Matt. Choosing not to become a pancake, Matt jumped to the side. Hulk lost his footing and hit the mat. The ground shook and the students laughed. Matt smiled weakly. Hulk snarled and leaped back up.

"Think dat was funny, Calhan?" he asked.

"I'm not sure how to answer that," Matt admitted.

Hulk rolled his head and cracked his neck, then charged at Matt again. Matt dodged him once more, but not before Hulk's arm caught Matt in the stomach. With an "oof!" Matt bent over and staggered back. Hulk charged him again and slammed into Matt's body, knocking him to the floor. The coach blew his whistle three times, waving his hands and stepping onto the mat.

"Stop! Stop! Stop!" he cried. "Okay, Hulk, this isn't WWE, remember? No chairs—no rough stuff. I'm giving Matt a point for your unnecessary roughness."

"Coach!" Hulk cried.

"And a caution."

"Coach!"

"You all right, Matt?"

"Pbbbbbppppttttttt," Matt said, his stomach aching.

"All right, get up and let's go again." He turned to Hulk. "Any more moves like that and you could lose by penalties."

Coach stepped back and blew his whistle.

"Matt, you're way ahead!" Gill shouted from the sidelines.

Hulk and Matt danced around in a circle for nearly fifteen seconds. Hulk charged Matt again. Matt, afraid of getting the "snot beat out of him" again, ran. And he *kept* running. He was ten feet away from the mat when Coach Plymouth blew his whistle. He gave Matt a penalty point for fleeing the mat, along with a caution.

Matt shot a quick glance at his gym bag. If there were just some way to get to the laptop. Just *some* way . . .

Suddenly, as if he heard Matt's mind begging, Coach said, "Um . . . Okay, boys, wait. Before we continue . . . I'm sorry. I've gotta hit the restroom. This water diet. Umph." And he headed toward the locker room.

"Me too!" Matt shouted, victoriously. At once, he ran to the side, grabbed his bag and followed Coach out of the gym.

## 9

# Strength

As fast as his legs would carry him, Matt ran into the locker room, right behind Coach Plymouth. The coach detoured toward the urinals; Matt grabbed a stall. He rushed inside, wrinkled his nose, and then sat on the edge of the seat. Matt threw his towel to the side of his bag, pulled the laptop out, opened it and pressed the power button. He waited for it to boot. He could hear Coach Plymouth on the other side of the door.

As Matt sat and waited, guilt washed over his body like a wave of the flu.

"It's all right to use the laptop so long as no one gets hurt," Sam had said.

Then Matt heard his own words: "I think *I'm* getting hurt."

"The laptop grasps you," Sam had added, "and won't let go."

"I'm not going to let it get hold of me like that," Matt had boldly proclaimed.

Matt gulped, staring at the computer in his lap. Suddenly, somehow, using the laptop didn't seem like such a good idea. And yet, if he didn't, Matt knew he'd be crushed out on the mat. There was no good way out of this. He just wasn't strong enough.

"It's not about strength," Alfonzo had said. "It's about smarts and speed. No strength is a match for good strategy."

Matt shook his head. It might be true, but he didn't know *any* strategy that would keep him from getting beat up. He needed an edge—an edge the laptop would give him.

Matt stared at the swirling Wordtronix logo. On the other side of the door, the coach was still going to the bathroom. He really *did* drink a lot of water.

Matt opened the word processor and placed his hands on the keyboard. He squeezed his eyes tightly, then typed:

```
Matt Calahan is a slick, well-oiled
wrestling machine. He surprised everyone
by winning the match against Hulk—and
making the team without one break, bruise
or scrape. He's Matt the Great! Matt the
Powerful! Matt the Great and Powerful!
```

Isabel had confided in Matt that "Alfonzo told me about what you said about how we need to live up to a higher standard, you know, since we're Christians now. You know, no lying, stuff like that."

*But what if I have no choice?* Matt argued with the memory. *What if there's no other way out of this?*

Matt placed his finger on top of the clock key, but didn't press down.

"The Truth will set you free," Pastor Ruhlen had said.

*But what's the truth?* Matt wondered.  *That I should take whatever pummeling I'm about to receive? That I'm about to break my arm? Or worse?*

"We're very proud of you," Matt's mother and father had said.

Matt couldn't get himself to press his finger down and make the laptop go to work.

"Stop it!" Matt said aloud, shouting to the memories in his head.

Suddenly, on the other side of the stall door, Coach Plymouth stopped doing what he was doing. "Sorry, Matt, but I gotta go."

"Not . . . not you," Matt called back. "Never mind."

Matt looked at his computer screen. There were the words in black and white:

> Matt Calahan is a slick, well-oiled wrestling machine. He surprised everyone by winning the match against Hulk—and making the team without one break, bruise or scrape. He's Matt the Great! Matt the Powerful! Matt the Great and Powerful!

All he had to do was press the clock key. One simple, little, harmless act and he'd make the team—safely. But he couldn't do it. Deep down, Matt knew it wasn't a harmless act. It was *wrong*. No, using the laptop wasn't wrong ... but using it *now* ... when he was grounded from it, was *wrong*. Matt looked up at the stained ceiling tiles. "I'm scared I'm going to die," Matt mumbled.

"The only one we should fear is God himself," preached Pastor Ruhlen days before, "respecting him as our King."

*Respecting God ... a higher standard*, Matt thought, looking up.

Then he brought his gaze down and looked at the paragraph he had written one more time. He took his finger off the clock key, slid his finger across the touchpad and closed the word processor on his laptop, erasing the story without activating it. Then he turned the computer off.

That was it.

Not enough time to go back now, even if he wanted to.

He had sealed his fate.

Matt realized that no matter how much he feared for his life, there was one thing he feared more: disrespecting God. And he didn't want to disrespect God by *not* living at that higher standard he held Alfonzo to ... the higher standard he held *himself* to. He had pushed the envelope enough by disobeying his parents. He couldn't do it any longer. No matter what. He would make it right as soon as he could.

Matt shivered, realizing his choice meant he was about to take the beating of his life and lose the match for sure. How much would Isabel lower her opinion of him when he showed up in a full body cast? One thing was certain: She probably wouldn't be waiting for him at her mailbox ever again.

Matt closed the laptop and slid it back into his gym bag. "God, just give me strength," he prayed. "That's all I ask for. Just give me strength to make it through this in one piece."

He waited for an answer, but didn't hear one.

"C'mon, Matt! Let's go!" Coach Plymouth barked, slapping the wall on his way out.

Matt exited the stall and washed his hands (it just seemed like the right thing to do). He walked back into the gym. As he entered, no one even seemed to notice. Matt's classmates just saw this as another run-of-the-mill bout, but he knew it was more. It was the end of weakling Matt Calahan. He stared at the ground as he walked, knowing he was about to go from the frying pan into the fire.

Matt stepped through his friends and dropped his gym bag by Alfonzo. Hulk, on the other side of the mat, wiped his face with his towel. Matt felt the sweat beading up on his forehead. He unzipped his gym bag and reached in for his own towel.

"Ouch!" Matt cried, pulling his hand out. A small paper cut left a tiny slice on his index finger. "What in the . . . ?" Matt reached into his bag to see what cut him. There, wrinkled at the bottom of his gym bag, was a small, double-folded piece of notebook paper—the note Isabel had given him the day before. Matt hadn't even bothered to read it. He pulled it out and opened it up. It said:

*Matt, here are some scriptures I looked up for you.* ☺

*I wrote them so you could say them to yourself when you're faced with a tough situation:*

1. *God did not give us a spirit of timidity, but a spirit of power, of love and of self-control. (2 Timothy 1:7)*
2. *There is no fear in love. (1 John 4:18)*
3. *Don't be afraid; just believe. (Mark 5:36)*
4. *So do not fear, for I am with you; do not be dismayed, for I am your God. (Isaiah 41:10)*
5. *The Lord is with me. I will not be afraid. (Psalm 118:6)*

*Anyway, I thought you would like these, because you're growing smarter, stronger, deeper, and cooler every day (Luke 2:52)—and they're the Truth!*

☺ *Isabel*

"Matt, you ready?" Coach Plymouth called.

Matt nodded. He reread the last phrase again. *They're the Truth.* He blinked. Pastor Ruhlen had said, "The Truth will set you free." He remembered Sam's monster story. Once she discovered the truth about the monster being a coat, all fear went away— the same way Matt's fear about Sam left him the more he got to know her.

"Matt?" Coach Plymouth called again.

*The Truth*, Matt read. "This is the Truth," he said aloud to no one in particular. *God hasn't given me a spirit of fear*, he realized, scanning the note. *He's given me power. He's driven fear out of me. God is with me. He's strengthening me and helping me.*

*The risk*, Matt realized, *was in trying to do this without him. Without* his *strength.*

"Matt, you all right?" Gill asked.

Matt folded up the paper and dropped it into his gym bag. In a daze, he turned around and stepped onto the mat, and into the competition area. And suddenly, like the fusing of a bomb, Matt felt a surge of energy—pure strength—shoot through his being. *The Lord is on my side. I will not fear!*

"Ready, punk?" Hulk challenged Matt.

Matt's eyes popped up to meet the challenge. He rolled his head and cracked his neck. "The question is, are you ready for *me?*"

Hulk's eyes grew wide. "Ya . . . all right, Calhan?"

Matt smiled. "I've never been more ready to have the snot beaten out of me."

Coach blew his whistle and Matt and Hulk continued the match. Before Hulk had a chance to think about coming at Matt, Matt charged Hulk at full speed, head first.

"Umph!" Hulk exclaimed, the air knocked out of him like a deflating balloon. He stared at Hulk; he had actually knocked him off his feet and slammed him onto the ground. Matt jumped on top of him, a new-found strength zipping through his veins. He used the surprise to his benefit and took the advantage.

"Takedown!" Coach shouted. "Two points for Matt!"

"Yeah!" Lamar, Gill, and Alfonzo screamed at the same time.

Matt tried pinning Hulk down, but the surprise was over. Hulk pushed back with every bit of might he had. With a roll, he knocked Matt off of him, turned his body sideways, and pulled his leg around Matt's. Matt flipped around and found himself underneath Hulk.

"Reversal! Two for Hulk!" Coach Plymouth noted, marking his pad.

They were now tied 3–3.

Hulk's eyes narrowed as he pressed down on Matt, trying to pin him to the mat. Matt turned his shoulders sideways.

"Go . . . down!" Hulk ordered Matt.

"I . . . loooooooovvvee . . . wrestling!" Matt grunted back.

Matt wiggled sideways, then worked his arm around Hulk's left arm. He pulled and pushed Hulk sideways. Hulk pushed back. Back and forth, Matt and Hulk wrestled, pushing and pulling, pulling and pushing. Hulk just couldn't get Matt pinned.

"Don't give up!" Lamar cheered from the sidelines.

"You can do it!" Alfonzo echoed.

"That's my boy!" Gill cried.

A minute later, time ran out, and Coach Plymouth blew his whistle.

*I did it!* Matt thought. *I'm still alive!!!*

"All right, guys! Great job!" Coach shouted.

The boys in the P.E. class clapped. Lamar, Gill, and Alfonzo hooted and hollered.

Hulk and Matt continued pushing against each other.

Coach Plymouth moved onto the mat. "Hulk, you can let go now. Hulk?"

"Um . . . it's . . . over," Matt said.

"But I haveta get him down!" Hulk moaned.

Coach Plymouth blew his whistle twice more, the second time into the big lug's ear. Hulk finally released his grip, and Matt collapsed onto the mat, flat on his back.

Hulk, sitting beside him, out of breath, and now a little hard-of-hearing, patted Matt on the shoulder. "Man . . . yer good, Calhan."

"Yes, indeed," Coach Plymouth said. "You both are. Welcome to the team, guys."

Staring up at the glaring gym lights, Matt smiled. A warm feeling rushed through his body; a satisfaction that no one could take away. He had tried his best and made the team. And though they tied, he actually stood his own against Hulk . . . without even getting a scratch.

Alfonzo jumped onto the mat and helped Matt up. As they walked off, two of their classmates entered the mat and started another match. Matt gave his friends high-fives.

"I *knew* you could do it!" Gill cheered.

"You made the team," Lamar congratulated Matt, "*without* the laptop." Then, "That *was* without the laptop, right?"

"It had to be," he answered. Then he turned to Alfonzo. "After all, I live to a higher standard."

Alfonzo smiled. "I think I'm starting to like these rules," he said. "Makes life a bit more challenging when you have something to shoot for."

"Tell me about it," Matt said with a laugh.

"Hey, man, I'm sorry I doubted you."

Matt shook his head. "In a way, I'm glad you did. I think I just needed someone to remind me that I could do it alone."

"Alone?" Lamar challenged Matt.

Matt looked up. "Well, no. Not entirely."

*Thank You, Lord*, he thought. *Thanks for the strength—just when I needed it.*

After school and several slaps on his back from his friends, Matt returned the laptop to its hibernating place. He exited his parents' room and headed toward his own. He jumped when his dad met him at the top of the stairs.

"Dad?!" Matt said. "I thought you were at work."

Mr. Calahan nodded. "I couldn't wait to hear. How did wrestling go?"

"I made the team."

"Atta' boy, Ace!" His dad laughed and messed up Matt's hair.

"Yeah."

"Hey," his dad said, following Matt into his bedroom, "maybe this will be your sport."

"I don't know about *that*...but maybe. I have a bunch of matches I'll have to be in now ... but it doesn't scare me. Not anymore."

"Well, I'm really proud of you."

Matt sat on the edge of his bed. His gut felt queasy.

After a pause, Matt's dad asked, "You all right, Ace?"

Matt said, "Well, um, here's the thing ..."

"Yes?"

"I know I wasn't supposed to, but I took the laptop out of the closet three times and used it to type some short stories—none of which were good and, in fact, I deleted the last one and then I put the laptop back and I never told you because I didn't want to get in trouble, but I didn't think I had a choice, but I did, and most of the time I felt it was truly a matter of life and death and you said it would be all right under those circumstances, but I have a feeling it wasn't *really* life and death, so I'm really sorry I disobeyed you and—"

Mr. Calahan put up his hand, his face drawn down in disappointment. Matt stopped speaking and waited for the anger, the punishment.

"Matt, you're a smart kid, right?"

He nodded and shrugged, waiting for the punchline.

"Matt, your mom and I have taken away your laptop for a reason. You need to realize there are other things in life you can enjoy, too. Now tell me, how in the world could *anything* become a matter of life and death with the laptop?"

With a gulp, Matt searched for the words. "I'm not sure how to answer that," he said truthfully.

"That's because there is no answer," Mr. Calahan said forcefully. "Unless you tell me it's some amazing device that has the ability to change the universe, there is no good answer, Matt."

Matt looked down.

Matt's dad took a deep breath. Sadness washed over his face. "One day, I'm going to find out what it is about that laptop that is such a draw to you. But until then, two more weeks. And to think you almost made it. It's disappointing."

Matt looked at the floor as his dad left the room.

After a moment, Matt popped his head back up, wanting to ask, "That's *it*?" But he knew that wasn't it. He had lost a bit of his parents' trust when he lied, and only gained a fraction of it back when he told the truth.

Matt shook his head. He wouldn't do it again, no matter *what* happened. *Stupid, stupid, stupid.*

Matt laid back on his bed and stared up at the ceiling. The whirlwind that was his life seemed to be spinning down for a short while anyway. And though he was grounded from his laptop—*again*—in some ways, he felt thankful. The discovery he had made about choosing whether to live *with* fear or *without* was a valuable one . . . one that even Sam herself had yet to figure out. And maybe, just maybe, Matt thought, he was the stronger for it.

# Epilogue

Sam handed Matt a small, rectangular card. "Here," she said, brushing back her blonde hair. "Put this into the side slot on your laptop."

"What's it do?" Matt asked.

"It's a wireless network card. This would have been easier had you brought the laptop."

"I told you," Matt said. "I'm grounded from it for two more weeks. And I'm not messing up again this time."

"Very well," Sam agreed. "We'll wait. But not too much longer before we do it."

"Do what?" Matt asked.

Sam smiled. "Everything."

**To be continued...**

# The Truth

Here are the scriptures Isabel looked up. They're written so you can say them to yourself when you're faced with a scary situation, too!

1. God did not give us a spirit of timidity, but a spirit of power, of love and of self-control. (2 Timothy 1:7)
2. There is no fear in love. (1 John 4:18)
3. Don't be afraid; just believe. (Mark 5:36)
4. So do not fear, for I am with you; do not be dismayed, for I am your God. (Isaiah 41:10)
5. The Lord is with me. I will not be afraid. (Psalm 118:6)

Don't ever forget them, because you're growing smarter, stronger, deeper, and cooler every day (Luke 2:52)—and they're the Truth!

# About the Author

For more than ten years, **Christopher P. N. Maselli** has been sharing God's Word with kids through stories. He is the author of multiple award-winning projects including an international children's magazine, a middle-grade adventure novel series, videos, and more.

Chris lives in Fort Worth, Texas, with his wife, Gena, and their feline twins, Zoë and Zuzu. He is actively involved in his church's KIDS Church program, and his hobbies include inline skating, collecting *It's a Wonderful Life* movie memorabilia and "way too much" computing.

# What is 2:52 Soul Gear™?

Based on Luke 2:52: "And Jesus grew in wisdom and stature, and in favor with God and men (NIV)," 2:52 Soul Gear™ is designed just for boys 8-12! This verse is one of the only verses in the Bible that provides a glimpse of Jesus as a young boy. Who doesn't wonder what Jesus was like as a kid?

The 2:52 Soul Gear™ takes a closer look by focusing on the four major areas of development highlighted in Luke 2:52:

- "Wisdom" = mental/emotional = **Smarter**
- "Stature" = physical = **Stronger**
- "Favor with God" = spiritual = **Deeper**
- "Favor with man" = social = **Cooler**

Become smarter, stronger, deeper, and cooler as you develop into a young man of God with 2:52 Soul Gear™!

Zonder**kidz**.

# Laptop 8: Shut Down!

**True Courage Reveals the Laptop's Truth**
**Written by Christopher P. N. Maselli**

laptop #8

## shut down!

True Courage Reveals
the Laptop's Truth

by Christopher P. N. Maselli

smarter • stronger
2:52
deeper • cooler

Zonder**kidz**

Softcover: 0-310-70667-X

Zonder**kidz**.

# Apprehensions

The inventor worked long and hard to destroy her own invention ... or at the very least, those who would misuse it. She knew eventually her rest would come. The question was: at what cost?

## Wednesday, 6:52 p.m.

"Your knee's shaking."

Matt stopped shaking his knee. "No, it's not."

Isabel Zarza stared Matt straight in the face. He looked away from her swallowing brown eyes.

"C'mon, Matt," Isabel pressed him, her voice sounding like newly-spun honey. "I know you. What's wrong?"

Matt's knee started shaking again.

*I'm just a bit on edge,* he wanted to say, *because this Saturday I'm going to more than just a wrestling tournament. I'm about to encounter a very dangerous situation because a mysterious woman I barely know but implicitly trust, asked me to. I'm Superman. Saving the world without anyone ever knowing it.*

Isabel let out a long breath. She looked across the room. Matt followed her gaze; their youth pastor was getting ready to start youth group. Matt loved youth group, and he loved talking to Isabel . . . but tonight he was, well, just a bit on edge. *All because I'm responsible for saving the world,* he thought again.

 "I know things will go fine at your tournament," Isabel encouraged him. "I'll even pray that God will give you strength just like before."

"Thanks," Matt said with a genuine smile. He wasn't afraid; that wasn't it. He just wasn't sure if he had what it would take to save the world. *That's kind of a heavy thing to lay on the shoulders of a thirteen-year-old,* Matt thought.

Isabel returned his smile, her eyes twinkling, but worry marks wrinkled her forehead. Matt hoped this wouldn't be the last time he saw her smile.

## Wednesday, 8:27 p.m.

"Your knee's shaking."

Matt stopped shaking his knee. "No, it's not."

Pastor Mick Ruhlen, youth pastor at Enisburg Community Church, stared Matt straight in the face. The youth service was over and Matt's stomach was still in knots. "What's going on, dude? You can tell me."

Matt sighed. *Not this time,* he thought. He looked at Pastor Ruhlen's chia-pet shaped hair up close. It was orange tonight.

"C'mon, dude," Pastor Ruhlen said emphatically. "I know you were hardly payin' attention during the service. That's not like my guy, Matt. What's wrong?"

Matt looked across the youth hall at bleach-blonde haired, 200-and-some-pound bully, Hulk Hooligan. The big lug had his hand under his shirt, making armpit noises.

"Why single *me* out?" Matt said defensively. "Hulk never listens."

"Right-e-o," Pastor Ruhlen agreed, laying his surfer-dude talk on thick. "But *you* do."

Matt shrugged. "I have a lot on my mind," he admitted. *For instance, what if this mission Sam roped us into doesn't go as planned? What if something goes wrong? What then? How will I handle it? And how will I forgive myself if the laptop gets into the wrong hands?*

"Well, friend," Pastor Ruhlen comforted, throwing a lanky arm around Matt's shoulders, "whatever it is, you can be sure that God will be with you."

"Yeah."

Pastor Ruhlen jumped up suddenly and ran to the podium at the front of the room. He grabbed his

# 2:52 Soul Gear™ Laptop fiction books—
## Technological thrillers that will keep you on the edge of your seat ...

**Laptop 1: Reality Shift**
They Changed the Future
Written by Christopher P. N. Maselli
Softcover 0-310-70338-7

**Laptop 2: Double-Take**
Things Are Not What They Seem
Written by Christopher P. N. Maselli
Softcover 0-310-70339-5

**Laptop 3: Explosive Secrets**
Not Everything Lost Is Meant to Be Found
Written by Christopher P. N. Maselli
Softcover 0-310-70340-9

**Laptop 4: Power Play**
Beware of Broken Promises
Written by Christopher P. N. Maselli
Softcover 0-310-70341-7

**Laptop 5: Dangerous Encounters**
Tangled Truths & Twisted Tales—Exposed!
Written by Christopher P. N. Maselli
Softcover: 0-310-70664-5

**Laptop 6: Hot Pursuit**
Steer Clear of "Golden" Opportunities
Written by Christopher P. N. Maselli
Softcover: 0-310-70665-3

**Laptop 8: Shut Down!**
True Courage Reveals the Laptop's Truth
Written by Christopher P. N. Maselli
Softcover: 0-310-70667-X

Available now at your local bookstore!

**Zonderkidz.**

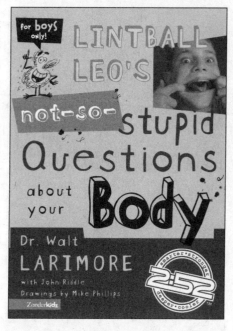

# Also from Inspirio

CD Holder
ISBN: 0-310-99033-5
UPC: 025986990336

Book & Bible Cover
Large  ISBN: 0-310-98824-1
       UPC: 025986988241
Med  ISBN: 0-310-98823-3
       UPC: 025986988234

inspirio

*The gift group of Zondervan*

We want to hear from you. Please send your comments about this book to us in care of zreview@zondervan.com. Thank you.

# Zonder**kidz**.

*Grand Rapids, MI 49530*
www.zonderkidz.com